The Vineyard in Crete

Richard Clark

Praise for Richard Clark's Books

'Clark is particularly good on the colours, flavours and scents of Greece. He has got under the skin of the place in a way few outsiders have been able to.'

Mark Hudson, winner of Somerset Maugham Award, Thomas Cook Travel Book Award and the Samuel Johnson Prize

'Richard Clark captures the spirit of Greece I love. His books make me long to see the places he describes.'

Jennifer Barclay, author of *Falling in Honey, An Octopus in My Ouzo, Wild Abandon* and *Taverna by the Sea*

'There is poetry in Richard Clark's words and through his eyes. I recommend anyone missing Greece, visiting Greece or just wishing they could go to Greece to take a look!'

Sara Alexi, author of *The Greek Village Series*

'Thanks, Richard, for adding your great eye to your gifted pen in service to sharing the essence of Greece with the world!'

Jeffrey Siger, bestselling, award-winning US crime writer

'Richard Clark writes with great authority and a deep affection for his subject, which comes from his long association with Greece… Excellent.'

Marjory McGinn, author of *The Peloponnese Series, A Saint for the Summer* and *How Greek is Your Love?*

'Return to Turtle Beach is a heart-warming story that will transport you to the enchanting island of Crete.'

Maria A. Karamitsos, *My Greek Books*

'In *The Forgotten Song* the author weaves his magical prose to take the reader on a romantic journey with more twists and turns than a Cretan mountain pass.'

Tony Prouse, author and journalist

'There are moments when this book [*The Crete Walking Society*] literally took my breath away! Sometimes with the beautifully captured images of Crete and sometimes the powerful feelings brought to life in the characters. Richard Clark is firmly one of my all-time favourite authors. His books are so beautifully written and an absolute joy to read.'

Angie Fox Lane

'Richard has a writing style that transports you to the real Greece. I truly love his ability to take me with him to wonderful places, feel the warmth of the Greek sunshine and experience Greece through the eyes of his characters. For me, he is one of the best writers out there.'

Peter Barber, author of *A Parthenon on Our Roof* and *A Parthenon in Pefki*

[*A Piano Bar in Crete*] is 'a poignant modern story, brilliantly crafted, with universal appeal.'

Suzi Stembridge, author

By the Same Author

A Piano Bar in Crete

The Crete Walking Society

The Forgotten Song

Return to Turtle Beach

The Lost Lyra

The Greek Islands – A Notebook

Crete – A Notebook

Rhodes – A Notebook

Corfu – A Notebook

Hidden Crete – A Notebook

More Hidden Crete – A Notebook

Eastern Crete – A Notebook

Richard Clark's Greek Islands Anthology

The Crete Trilogy

The Vineyard in Crete

First published in America and Great Britain 2024

Copyright © Richard Clark 2024

Cover design © Mike Parsons 2024

All rights reserved. No part of this publication can be reproduced or transmitted in any form or by any means, electronic or mechanical, without permission in writing from Richard Clark.

Richard Clark has asserted his right to be identified as the author of this work in accordance with the Copyright, Designs and Patents Act, 1988

ISBN – 9798326429193

www.facebook.com/richardclarkbooks

https://notesfromgreece.com

About the Author

Richard Clark is a writer, editor and journalist who has worked on an array of national newspapers and magazines in the UK. In 1982, on a whim, he decided to up sticks and live on the Greek island of Crete. So began a love affair that has continued to this day, and he still visits the Greek islands, where he has a home, on a regular basis. In 2016, he gave up the daily commute to London to become a full-time author. He is married with two grown-up children and five grandchildren, and lives in Kent.

Acknowledgements

This book is a work of fiction, and although some real places have lent themselves as locations, many are the product of my imagination. All the characters are fictitious, and any resemblance to real persons, living or dead, is purely coincidental. Any mistakes are mine.

A huge thank you goes to Tony and Bernadette Prouse for reading each chapter as it was produced and for their guidance. I am also grateful to the author Yvonne Payne for reading and giving her comments on the manuscript.

As always, I am lucky to be edited by the patient and meticulous Jennifer Barclay who has made this book better than it otherwise might have been. Again I am grateful to Mike Parsons for his beautiful cover design. Lastly, I must thank my family, Denise, Rebecca, James, Pete, Lucy, Esther, Imogen, Iris, Douglas and Edward for their unending support.

Note

The names of male Greek characters ending in an 's' will drop the letter in the vocative case (when that character is being addressed in direct speech).

To Petra

Thank you for finding me a vineyard

Part 1

1971

Chapter 1

THROUGH THE SHUTTERS, Sofia could sense the sun setting. Maybe it would bring some relief from the stifling heat in the room in which she had been locked for two days now. She heard footsteps approaching; her father entered, noisily putting a plate of horta and rusks and a glass of water down on the table.

It would be no good trying to reason with him. He was like a brooding bull always ready to charge. She watched him but sat perfectly still, knowing he would find it impossible to forgive her. His anger would also make any attempt to escape fruitless. He wordlessly left, slamming the door and turning the key. She felt the bruises around her wrists and willed herself to stop shaking.

Sofia had run out of tears. She thought she was in love with Michalis, but why had she been so stupid as to let her father catch them together? She worried for her mother. Her father was more than capable of taking out his fury on his wife.

As Tassos returned to the kitchen, he felt no compassion for his daughter, despite the deep brown eyes that had stared at him when he took her food. Since her birth, she had progressed from being an inconvenience and financial burden to now disgracing him. In the shadows of his dark mind a plot began to form that would avenge the shame. A smirk turned up the corners of his mouth.

Dimitra made as if to say something to her husband after she heard him lock the bedroom door again, then she thought better of it and busied herself preparing supper. She was distraught that the cruelty with which he had always treated her had now grown to embrace their daughter Sofia. Yet she had learned not to cross this beast of a man; any questioning his actions she knew would only make matters worse.

She looked at his short, stocky frame as he sat at the table drinking raki. For years there had been little room inside him for anything but resentment. His face was set in a grim smile and she feared the thoughts which simmered behind his fixed gaze. Pouring wine from a plastic barrel into a large metal jug, she took the chicken and potatoes from the oven and put them on a plate, adding some boiled mountain greens from the pan on the hob. She neither expected nor got any thanks as she placed the meal in front of him. His rheumy eyes were glazed, staring into the half-distance.

Dimitra held no grudge against her father for her arranged marriage or *synikasio*. Her parents had been poor in those hardest of times in the wake of the Second World War and the Civil War that followed. After her mother's death giving birth to her sister, her father had little dowry to offer with her hand in marriage, and when a less than scrupulous *proxenitis* or matchmaker had found a man with some land willing to take her, it was considered an advantageous union. At seventeen, she had been little more than a child when she had left Loutro.

After her move to these mountains above the small village of Epano Elounda at the other end of the island, it soon became apparent that her new husband wanted nothing but a slave to cook and clean for him. Tassos had not even allowed her to return home for her sister's wedding or her father's funeral. He was aggressive and lazy, and the small plot of land put down to grapevines was neglected, bringing in just enough money to keep him in drink and food and, with careful management, allow an existence for herself and Sofia.

Her heart broke at the thought of her only child locked in a bedroom. When she had fallen pregnant not long after their marriage, she had prayed that the birth of their child would bring them closer together. That had been a forlorn hope. The presence of another mouth to feed had only worsened her husband's angry behaviour. As the years passed, he drank more and more, and became increasingly violent.

Dimitra caught herself in the mirror which hung on the wall in the living area. She thought she had shrunk, she looked tired, her hair was turning grey but her brown eyes, although sunken, still burned bright as they stared back at her.

She escaped the poisoned atmosphere of the house, and went outside to the comfort of the ever-present rickety chair beside the back door. She sat down and stared out across the overgrown vineyard. The sun glowed orange as it met the mountains, the sky turning from crimson to purple as the light began to fade. Her eyes alighted on the neat, spaced-out rows of vines spread across the hillside beyond, a stark contrast to the haphazard planting on her husband's land.

'That fool Christos will never make any money. He thinks he is in France or somewhere,' she remembered Tassos saying, laughing about his neighbour's meticulous planting high on this Cretan mountainside. 'Better to get as many plants into the space and grow as many grapes as you can. The cooperative doesn't mind what they taste like, they pay by quantity. The wine's good enough for me to drink so it should be for everyone else!'

But as the years went by, the yield from their vineyard had dropped. The grapes were smaller, more bitter and harder to harvest, and Dimitra suspected that her husband's reluctance to replicate the beautiful symmetry of his neighbour's vineyard had more to do with indolence than any well thought-out business plan.

'What are you doing idling your time away sitting there?' Tassos did not wait for an answer from his wife. 'I'm off to Elounda for a drink.'

Tassos made his way, as he did several times a week, along the path which ran down the mountain to the hillside village of Epano Elounda, where the trail met the alleyways meandering between the houses. He slunk past the local taverna, already half full of his neighbours eating mezzes and drinking wine and raki.

He would not be welcome there. He heard laughter through the windows and quickened his step to reach the donkey track leading down towards the sea.

Four years earlier, he had been hopeful when the military coup had overthrown the government. But while he may have supported the fascists, in his more lucid moments he had to admit that since they had come to power, his life had not improved. He consoled himself in the knowledge that for many of those in the surrounding villages, things had got much worse. Most of the villagers hated being under the yoke of the military regime but the reign of terror, of torturing and murdering any who were suspected of opposing the Junta's rule, kept resistance under cover. Everyone knew of someone who had disappeared, and the secret police had eyes and ears everywhere.

Entering the small town of Elounda, Tassos made his way towards a dimly lit drinking hole on the square. Two police cars were parked outside. As he entered, the four officers at the bar nodded. Several other tables were taken up mostly with office workers, functionaries of the state on their way home from work. He approached the counter and ordered a karafaki of raki, taking it to a table at the back of the bar. The policemen laughed loudly but the rest of the customers were quiet, the only other sound that of hushed conversations or the click of a tavli counter slammed down on a board.

Tassos poured a glass of the clear liquid. He lifted it to his lips and took a sip. The fiery spirit warmed his throat and he smiled at the familiar comfort he felt inside. As he drank, the vague plot he had been forging in his head began to take shape. By the time he returned to the bar to order his second karafaki he had convinced himself to pursue a dark course of action. He thought about returning to his land right away and seizing the moment, but he was enjoying his drink and wanted a clear head to execute the retribution he had craved since he was a child.

*

Two days before, he had been sitting outside his house, staring down the mountainside towards the bay in the distance. The olive trees waved in the breeze. Why had he not grown olives like everyone else, instead of competing with his neighbour to grow vines? The land had been known to produce only low-quality grapes to make village wine at best.

But Panagiotis' vines were flourishing, whilst his own crop was getting smaller every year. Panagiotis' land must be better quality. Looking out across the plot his parents had left him on their death, the sense of injustice turned to anger. Seething with resentment, his eyes came to rest on a couple stealing a kiss between the rows of vines on his neighbour's land. It took him little more than a second to recognise his own daughter with the neighbour's son, Michalis.

Something in him snapped and he charged down the hill, stumbling over rocks that had not been cleared from the parched earth and pushing aside the tangle of vines which spread untended across his land. Puffing and panting, he scaled the drystone wall which divided his property from his neighbour's.

By the time the young couple spotted him, it was too late to run. They stood, frozen by fear. As Tassos approached, Michalis dropped his girlfriend's hand only for her father to grab it and pull her behind him.

'How could you!' Tassos screamed at his daughter. 'How could you even go near the family who were responsible for the death of your grandparents?'

Michalis did not know what Tassos was talking about but was shocked at the ferocity of the bitterness which poured from him. The anger written on Sofia's father's face was terrifying. As his vehemence reached fever pitch, Michalis noticed balls of spit had formed at the corners of Tassos' distorted mouth, and fear told him to hold his silence.

'You will pay for this. And if you go near my daughter again, I will kill you.' For a moment Tassos held Michalis' eyes in his.

The young man was in no doubt that Sofia's father was not to be messed with. He felt a chill run through him as Tassos turned and walked back towards his own land, dragging his silent daughter behind him.

Tassos gripped Sofia's wrist hard as he pulled her over the wall and through the overgrown vines to the house, not speaking a word. Dimitra made to stand from the chair outside the back door, but seeing the look on her husband's face she thought better of it as he hauled Sofia inside the house and into her bedroom, slamming the door and locking it.

For some time Michalis stood rooted to the spot. He loved Sofia, but had been too frightened of her father to utter a word or move in her defence.

'Are you OK?' Michalis heard the reassuring voice of his father behind him. 'What's going on?' Panagiotis could usually see himself in his son: both were tall, though the younger man less muscular, and usually had a confident manner. Now all he saw was fear, confusion and sadness on his face. He put a hand on his shoulder and they sat down in the shade of the row of vines. As his son revealed what had happened and the threats Tassos had made, Panagiotis tried to make light of the situation. Inside, however, he was only too aware of his neighbour's unpredictability, particularly when he had been drinking.

*

Now, as Tassos walked back up the mountainside two days later, occasionally losing his footing on the loose rocks of the donkey track, his scheme began to take shape. He would teach his neighbours a lesson. It was time; and under the Junta, no-one would take the word of a democrat family against that of a supporter of the military regime. He had a plan that would ease his money problems, avenge his daughter's affair and bring retribution for the pain he had suffered all his life.

He stayed in the shadows as he passed the village taverna, where the sound of lyra and guitar wove around the song of contented chatter. To a man, he knew that the villagers hated the regime that held sway, so how was it that they could still find happiness whilst he lived from hand to mouth, every day a struggle to put food on the table or a drink in his belly? Well, that was all going to change.

Consumed by his thoughts, he continued through the darkened alleys to the top of the village and onto the path up the mountain. Under a full moon he could make out the evenly spaced rows of vines on the hillside. Beneath the vineyard he could see his neighbours' pristine, whitewashed farmhouse and the neat sugar cubes of the winery outbuildings round the courtyard. He felt the envy rise inside him. His neighbours were three generations of men working the land whilst he had lost his parents as a child and now had two useless women to feed. Bristling with anger, he skirted the boundary then hurried past his own fields before reaching the gap in the wall which led to his silent house.

*

The next day, as he did most Sundays, Christos invited the three generations of his family to visit a friend he had fought with during the war who owned a vineyard in the Archanes area near the island capital of Heraklion. In the front, Panagiotis drove, while Christos sat in the back of the car alongside his wife Maria. Her once jet-black hair was now grey, but to him she was as beautiful as the day he first saw her. She had been his rock throughout the war and the hard times since. He loved her now more than ever. Beside her sat their grandson, Michalis. How like his father he was; tall and strong with an open face.

His mind drifted back to the days and years following the war. He had needed to rebuild his livelihood from nothing. When hostilities had ceased, Christos had returned from the mountains with Maria and ten-year-old Panagiotis to their land above Epano Elounda and was welcomed as a hero by most of the other villagers. His land had been ravaged by the elements in his absence and stripped bare of any crops by the starving villagers. He would need to start again to build his business; but instead of returning to the way his farm had been, he had a strange vision. When the other villagers heard of his plans they thought he was mad, but he was an intelligent man and his status meant that most were prepared to indulge him and even help him to live his dream.

During the war Christos had encountered other freedom fighters from across the island: from Chania in the west, Sitia in the far east, and the land around Heraklion and the ancient Minoan city of Knossos. On cold nights, sitting around fires in caves, they had told each other of the lives they led in their villages. Many farmed olives, were fishermen, shepherds and goat herders or grew fruit and vegetables, some even were priests, but what had caught Christos' imagination had been the few men he encountered who cultivated vines to produce wine. In his village he knew some farmers made wine for their own consumption and for the local tavernas. But what inspired him was the romance of an art which stretched back to pre-Minoan times and was now practiced in places like France and Italy.

It would take patience to fulfil his dream but he had time and, most importantly, was still alive. Three years was how long it took before a vine might yield usable grapes, and five before they reached their full potential. He also needed to experiment as to what grapes would grow best in his soil and in what position on his plot. In the early days he travelled the island with his donkey, leaving Maria and Panagiotis at home, whilst he collected vines from comrades he had met in the resistance.

As Panagiotis grew up, he had worked hard helping Christos clear the land, and together they had dug and trellised it. Panagiotis had kept a notebook in which he mapped out the whole of the proposed vineyard, how much sun and wind each area was exposed to and the type and quality of the soil. Each time his father brought home a new vine, Panagiotis would mark on his plan where, when and the variety of grape they had planted.

Christos had built two *patitiria*, the presses where the grapes would be stomped, one for red varieties and one for yellow. After nurturing the precious crop, that first harvest had been modest, but the wine it produced had been of good quality and they were able to then select vines which were most suited to the land and which would make the best tasting wines. In the years that followed, they propagated those favoured varieties, replacing those less suited to the soil.

From the start Christos had been fixed on making his own wine rather than send his crop to the cooperative, so with the vines establishing themselves on the mountainside, he turned his attention to the winery. The outhouses were converted into spaces to press, mature and store the wine prior to its sale.

Now, Panagiotis had taken over much of the running of the vineyard. The rigours of the privations of the war years, with frozen nights sleeping rough on mountainsides, exacerbated by the following years spent swinging a pick and shovel and bending to tend his crop, began to take its toll on Christos' body. Arthritis had crept up on him, and he was more than happy to take a step back. Panagiotis loved to be out in all weathers working their vineyard and was fascinated by the alchemy of winemaking.

Christos was proud of his son, and could see that under Panagiotis' careful stewardship, the wine business he had worked so hard to set up was in safe hands. He was grateful of the way his son would indulge him when he offered up suggestions, and Panagiotis had taken the vineyard from strength to strength. In the passenger seat was Panagiotis' wife Calliope, a strong woman who made his son happy and whose laughter could brighten the darkest of days. He appreciated how they looked after Maria and himself.

The lunches were long, and the men would spend hours talking about wine, and drinking it. This particular summer Sunday was no different. Whilst they feasted on lamb shank, slowly roasted with oregano and thyme in the outside wood oven in the corner of the winery courtyard, they talked of the bumper crop they hoped to harvest the following month. Spring had been late, the rains lasting into the last days of May, and the summer had been hot, yet with afternoon breezes to stop the grapes from scorching. Their crops should be abundant and of high quality and both families were optimistic about the new blends of wine they hoped to produce that year.

It was late in the afternoon by the time they finished lunch. Calliope, as she did every Sunday, offered to drive as the men had been enjoying the produce of the vineyard. They dropped down the hillside from Archanes towards the sea before taking the national highway which snaked through the small seaside settlements beginning to develop along the coast. Not long after they had passed the monastery of St George near the top of the gorge of Selinari, she turned onto the winding road which cut across the mountains towards their home. As soon as they reached the summit, the view of the bay which usually greeted them was now blighted by black smoke, and it took only seconds for Panagiotis to realise it was coming from their land.

*

The acrid smell of smoke blew in on the breeze through the open door as Dimitra stood by the kitchen sink. Her eyes and throat began to itch as she crossed the room. Staring down the hillside she could see a fire had taken hold on the neighbours' land. Below the rows of vines, the farmhouse and winery were already ablaze and the flames were spreading up the mountainside.

Scanning the hills, she noticed something else. Behind the wall that separated their property from the neighbours', the straggling vines on their side had been cut down, and she could see water flowing from a disconnected irrigation pipe onto the usually parched, newly cleared earth. Her eyes followed the line of the boundary and alighted on the unmistakable figure of her husband, standing, watching the tragedy unfold.

For minutes Dimitra stood staring at the man she had been forced to marry, had never loved and had grown to hate. She watched him bend down, pick up a can, turn and begin to walk up the hillside towards the house.

She had no more than ten minutes. Rushing back inside, she turned the key in the door of Sofia's bedroom.

'Hurry, you must go now,' Dimitra shouted to her scared daughter, returning to the kitchen and pulling open a drawer to find the tin where she knew her husband kept his cash. Scribbling a note on a piece of paper she handed it, together with the stash of notes, to Sofia, who was still in her room.

'Take this and go. That's the name of my sister's village in Sfakia. She will look after you. I will follow when I can. We must get away. He won't realise you're missing until tonight when he brings you food. It will give you a head start to get away.'

'And what about you? He'll kill you if he finds out you let me go!'

Dimitra picked up the chair on which her daughter had been sitting and with surprising strength raised it above her head and smashed through the small window.

'He'll think that you broke the glass and escaped. Now come, you must go. Take the path into the mountains towards Neapoli, catch a bus west to Chania. You can then work out how to cross to the south.' Dimitra pulled her daughter through the bedroom door, locking it behind them.

For a moment Sofia stopped at the front door and raised a hand. 'Take care, mother.'

'Go! Now!'

Dimitra watched as her daughter disappeared up the track into the mountains. Within moments she was swallowed up by the landscape, but the walk to Neapoli was long and she must buy Sofia as much time as she could.

When Tassos entered the house he couldn't hide his self-satisfaction. He was happier than Dimitra had seen him in years. Every few minutes he could not stop himself from going outside and watching the fire move up the mountain, consuming Christos' vineyard. Watching from inside, she felt sick to her stomach seeing the fixed grin on her husband's face as he stared at the human chain of villagers trying to douse the flames. Her impulse was to help, but she knew this was impossible. Tassos could hardly contain his pride when the wind died just as the inferno reached the boundary wall.

'What are you staring at? The show's over.' Tassos sat down on the chair outside the door. 'Bring me a drink.' Dimitra went inside and poured a karafaki of raki, putting it with a glass on the table.

'Aren't you going to make me some food? I'm going to need all my strength if I've got to clear all our new land.' Dimitra couldn't help but look questioningly into the face of her husband. 'You heard me. They won't be coming back. I've seen to that. All that land is now mine for the taking. What are you staring at, get me some food! Whilst you're at it, put some rusks on a plate for your slut of a daughter. I'll deal with her after I've eaten.'

Dimitra lingered over the preparation of the salad she was making to accompany the goat stew which had been simmering on the stove for hours. She wanted to give Sofia chance to make her escape and delay the inevitable wrath of Tassos when he discovered she had gone.

Tassos took his time eating supper, and demanded his wife bring him more raki as he sat enjoying the spectacle unfolding in the neighbouring fields. He congratulated himself that no firefighters had come to the aid of the villagers. He had friends in high places, and had ensured that his neighbours themselves would be blamed for starting a dangerous wildfire.

It was dark by the time Tassos turned his mind to Sofia. Perhaps he should release his daughter and let her witness the destruction of her boyfriend's family's land. He stood and went inside, picking up the plate of rusks and glass of water his wife had put aside as he had instructed. Turning the key, he opened the door on the darkened room. It took only seconds for his eyes to adjust and to see the broken window. Smashing the plate and glass on the floor he turned on his wife.

'Did you not hear the glass break?' He raised his hand to strike her as he had so often before. This time something stopped him. Sofia's leaving was far greater punishment to this woman who had been nothing but a burden to him since their marriage. The loss of her daughter would cause her far more pain than anything he could inflict and, with the girl gone, there was one less mouth to feed.

Dropping his hand to his side he said nothing, but in that moment Dimitra saw evil cross his face and it scared her more than ever before. She knew that she must also escape. It was only a matter of time before he discovered the empty tin and would realise she had tricked him. Even if he was pleased that Sofia had left, he would never forgive the loss of his money. For that she would take a severe beating, or worse. With her daughter gone, she had nothing to stay for.

Tassos pushed past his wife, took the plastic container of raki from the kitchen shelf and returned outside. Tonight he would celebrate. Soon he would take possession of his neighbour's superior land, grow more vines and make more money. The villagers would not dare question his right to the land for fear of reprisals, and with Sofia gone too, his cash would go further.

As night fell, Tassos could still see the flames dancing over the vineyard below, illuminating the villagers desperately trying to douse the fire. By the time they had succeeded in putting a halt to the conflagration he was fast asleep, the empty container fallen on the floor beside him.

Dimitra seized her chance. Hastily she packed some food and drink from the store cupboard and crept out the door past her snoring husband. She did not want to go down the mountainside for fear of being seen by the villagers, so turned towards the mountain path which her daughter had taken that afternoon. It had been years since she had followed this track, but the moon was full and her need to get away had focused her mind. Even if Tassos did awaken soon, he would be in no fit state to follow her along the uneven path.

*

It was nearly midnight by the time the blaze was brought under control. Out on their feet, their blackened bodies covered in sweat, the bedraggled men made their way back down to the village. The owner of the taverna, who had been helping to fight the fire, opened his doors to the men, some of whom had come up from the coast to do what they could.

Panayiotis and his son Michalis sat among them, speechless. As they had approached the vineyard that afternoon, willing the car to go faster as Calliope swung around the hairpin bends, their worst fears were confirmed. The fire was destroying everything.

The land was ablaze, whilst their house and the winery they had so lovingly built over the years were engulfed in flames. The roof had fallen in and the old wooden brandy barrels they had imported from France in which to age that year's red vintage added more fuel to the inferno.

They had rushed to join their neighbours in trying to quench the flames. Christos had to be restrained from joining them, and eventually was persuaded to go to the village, where he, Maria and Calliope were given shelter whilst the younger men fought the fire. A man had run down the donkey track to Elounda to raise the alarm, but no help from firefighters or the police had been forthcoming. The fire had spread uphill on the afternoon sea breeze. The wind had dropped as dusk fell and the fire had halted at the wall between their land and Tassos' neighbouring plot.

As the crowd sat drinking joylessly, the door of the taverna opened to a breathless man familiar as a friend to many. He had come from the town with news he had heard from a young policeman: in the morning, the police would be coming to the village to arrest Christos and Panagiotis for the serious crime of starting a dangerous fire. A murmur passed through the villagers. Although they were trumped-up charges, all knew that the authorities would dispense with the inconvenience of a trial to prove the guilt of two known democrats, and they would be slung in jail at best.

Panagiotis turned to his son. 'We must leave now'. With little time to spare, the family had to escape that night. While Panagiotis went to collect Christos, Maria and Calliope, the taverna owner hurriedly prepared food and drink for them to take on their journey into the mountains.

Christos stood for a moment and looked at the blackened, scorched earth where his vineyard had flourished. He knew that his dream was over.

Chapter 2

IT TOOK SOFIA hours to reach the top of the mountains before beginning the winding descent towards Neapoli. She was grateful for the full moon as it meant she could stay on the mountain tracks rather than take to the roads where she was more likely to be seen. She thought about her mother left alone with her brute of a father, and about Michalis.

She reminisced about how they had grown up together, going to the same school in the village. They would walk home through the olive groves to the vineyards. As they moved into their teenage years they became closer. During the long summer months when they were not at school she would secretly watch him from a distance working in his grandfather's fields and yearn to hear his laughter. As they grew up, their relationship got closer and it was almost inevitable that they would become a couple. Now, her heart broke to think she would never see him again.

It was the early hours by the time she reached the outskirts of the town. Making her way through the deserted streets she found the main square, at the heart of which was a tranquil garden. There would be no bus west until the following day, the night was hot and she was ready to drop. She found a bench beneath the trees, folded the small bag she had been clutching, put it under her head and fell asleep.

*

'We have at best until morning before the police start looking for us,' said Panagiotis, driving through the dark across the mountains. 'But what then?'

'We can't just disappear, even in Heraklion,' said Christos from the back seat. 'With the secret police on the lookout, it will only be a matter of time before we are captured.'

They were known opposers of the regime and, although it was their home and livelihoods which had been destroyed by the fire, they were well aware that the blaze would be used as a pretext to arrest the whole family. They needed to get out of the country, but there was no way to board a ship or aeroplane without detection. Panagiotis' mind was racing but no answers were forthcoming.

Christos leaned forward as they approached the main national road. 'They'll assume we are heading to Heraklion. We should go east instead. I have old comrades in Sitia. It might buy us some time.'

Panagiotis turned the car in the direction of Agios Nikolaos. He trusted his father and realised that the friendships he had forged during the war might be their only hope of survival. The road made its way to the coast and they quickly navigated the familiar villages of Ammoudara and Kalo Chorio.

On the back seat Maria snored, her head rested against Michalis' shoulder. The moon cut a slice out of the dark sea and Christos stared out towards the horizon and wondered if he would ever see his home again. Turning his gaze inland he caught the shadowy outline of the remains of the ancient Minoan town of Gournia. He had to force himself to stop thinking of his vineyard razed to the ground, everything he had worked for to build a life for his family destroyed.

As they descended to sea level again, they left the Dikti Mountains behind before climbing into the Tripti range heading further east. The road got steeper and Panagiotis was forced to slow on the serpentine route which wove its way through the mountains. Somewhere below them was Mochlos and further on the Richtis Gorge. At last, the road dropped steeply down into the silent, darkened outskirts of Sitia. Christos directed them through the narrow streets.

It took some minutes to rouse his old comrade Vassilis to answer his door in the dark of the night. Once inside, the family was invited to sit around the kitchen table as Christos told his friend of their ordeal and the danger they were now in.

'You have to leave the country as soon as possible. Costa! Costa! Get down here now.' Seconds later a second man of about Panagiotis' age, short but muscular with a full black beard, came down the stairs.

'This is my son.' Costas nodded his head in recognition of the guests as his father quickly explained their predicament. 'Go to the harbour and find Petros.' He turned to Christos. 'You'll remember him from the war. I'm sure he will get you off the island.'

Costas was gone, slipping out into the darkness and the narrow streets which led to the harbourfront. When he emerged onto the esplanade he could see the large caique moored alongside the wall jutting out into the sea. A knock on the wheelhouse door brought the elderly captain from below, still bleary from sleep. Within minutes a plan had been formed. The captain drove to his yard where he loaded his truck with cans of diesel and other provisions to stow aboard.

Christos and his family set out on foot for the port, Vassilis agreeing to dispose of the car to hide their trail. By the time they reached the quayside, the engines were running ready for departure. Greeting his friend with a whisper, Petros ushered the family aboard and below into the cabin before casting off his lines. He stepped into the wheelhouse and eased the craft away from the harbour wall.

In the rush to leave, Christos had had little time to take in the plan which had been so quickly formed by Petros. But he knew he could trust his old comrade. He looked up through the hatch at the clear blue sky emerging from the darkness which signalled the start of a new life. He longed to go up on deck, but Petros insisted they stay below until they were well clear of land and could not be spotted.

The sea was smooth as glass. The family sat below deck – Christos and Maria, Panagiotis and Calliope and young Michalis – trying to take in what had happened. It was clear that they could not stay in Greece, even if they got far away from Crete. It would be difficult for them all to hide, and even if they could find refuge, their lives would be spent in constant fear of capture.

At the wheel, Petros felt the adrenaline in his blood, something he had not experienced since the war had ended some quarter of a century earlier. As the coast of Crete became a silhouette on the horizon he turned the helm west, parallel to the distant land and glanced at the compass, taking a bearing. The family was relieved to climb up out of the heat of the cabin. Petros handed the wheel to Panagiotis, giving him the course to hold, Michalis by his father's side, whilst Calliope took Maria to the cockpit at the stern. Petros disappeared below, emerging with a handful of charts, which he spread out on the table in the wheelhouse. Taking a pencil, a parallel rule and dividers, he drew on the charts, plotting their route.

*

Sofia awoke exhausted and aching. The realisation of what had happened came flooding back and she wanted to cry but fought back the tears, not wanting to draw attention to herself.

She left the garden, crossed the road and bought a bus ticket for Heraklion. There she could change for the bus towards Chania; the woman in the office told her she could get off at Vrysses then catch a local service through the mountains to Chora Sfakion. From there she could take a ferry along the coast to where her aunt lived in Loutro.

That early in the day there were plenty of seats, and Sofia found herself a place towards the back of the bus. The driver got on, started the engine, crossed himself and began to pull away.

Suddenly he applied the brakes and re-opened the doors. Sofia's heart froze as the fear of being caught engulfed her.

Then a bedraggled figure climbed aboard, whom she instantly recognised as her mother. She was flooded with relief. As Dimitra thanked the driver for stopping, she saw her daughter, and her face crumpled as she slumped down into the seat beside her. In tears, the women held each other tight.

The road hugged the coast and as the sun rose higher above the sea, mother and daughter's spirits began to rise too, knowing they were putting more and more distance between themselves and the man who had for so long made their lives intolerable. There was a niggling worry in both their minds that he might come after them, but in their hearts they knew he would not bother. For him life would be cheaper without them and he would be too lazy to follow.

In Heraklion they changed buses. The national highway left the city, rising into the undulating hills, playing hide and seek with the sea which revealed itself benignly calm whenever the road met the edge of the cliffs. The sky matched the intensity of the water before the sun reached its zenith and bleached it white.

The heat was uncomfortable at the village of Vrysses as they awaited the local bus which would take them from the north to the south coast of the island.

The bus rattled around the precarious bends into the White Mountains, and they were grateful to feel the temperature drop as the road steepened and they climbed higher. They passed through remote villages but mostly the land was desolate and it was hard to see how anyone could make a living from farming on the steep slopes. They passed the mouth of the Imbros Gorge, a vast canyon cut from the limestone rock. As they spiralled down the mountainside the views of the sea were spectacular, the ultramarine water getting closer and closer until they arrived in the isolated community of Chora Sfakion.

From the square it was a short walk to the harbour. Their destination could not be reached by road, the only access to the village of Loutro being by boat or on foot across the mountains. The ticket booth was closed and a faded timetable taped to the window revealed they would need to wait two hours for the passenger ferry which would take them on the last leg of their journey. They walked along the seafront past a memorial to those who had fallen here during the Second World War, and found a kafenio where they could sit and drink a coffee to while away the time. The café owner at first eyed them with suspicion and could not help but ask where they were from and Sofia could sense the emotion in her mother as she talked about returning home to Loutro after so long.

*

Christos stared over his old comrade's shoulder at the charts showing the vast expanses of sea they would be travelling. To port, on the horizon, the dark outline of his homeland. Ahead, a sea so vast and deep it looked as though it could go on forever.

The plan was to follow the coast of Crete westwards to the end of the island before heading north to Antikythera and Kythira, then to the Ionian Islands and Corfu before crossing the Adriatic to Italy, where it was hoped they would find asylum.

The thought came to him that he might never see Crete again, and he felt his eyes moisten. He sniffed and told himself he had faced far worse during the war, but that was when he was young; now he was a grandparent, his body weakened by the passage of time. Would he have the strength to begin again? He looked at Petros, poring over his charts, savouring the demands of the voyage, and he took strength from his friend.

'How long will we be at sea?' he asked.

Petros straightened and turned towards him. He could see the foreboding in Christos' eyes. He encircled his friend in a sturdy arm to reassure him. 'By dawn tomorrow we'll be off the western tip of Crete near Gramvousa. I made radio contact with some fishermen friends who'll meet us offshore and supply us with more cans of fuel and food and other provisions. The forecast is good; I don't think it should take much longer than four days to reach Salento. Hey, the sun will be shining, enjoy the trip.'

Despite his worries, Christos was encouraged by his old friend's relish at the adventure, and he told himself he must stay strong for his family, who would depend on his fortitude in the uncertain times which lay ahead.

'Thank you,' Christos said, looking into his friend's eyes to show how deeply he meant it. He glanced through the wheelhouse window. In the cockpit were his wife, grandson and daughter-in-law. 'I'll see if Maria needs to rest – she's been up all night.'

'Take her to my cabin at the stern, Christo. I can sleep up here by the wheel and the others can bed down in the saloon. Overnight you can share the watches with Panagiotis, Michalis and myself. If you all stick to the compass bearings I set you, we'll be fine.'

Christos nodded agreement, stepped out onto the deck and made his way to the cockpit. 'Maria, you must be exhausted. Let me show you where we will be sleeping.' He helped his wife to her feet, leading her through the wheelhouse down the companionway below deck and to the comfort of Petros' cabin. 'Try to get some rest.' Christos kissed his wife on the forehead. Looking down at the woman he loved, he saw that she was already sound asleep.

Calliope too went below and lay down to sleep on one of the benches. With Panagiotis at the wheel and Petros busy with his chartwork, Christos sat alone with his grandson in the cockpit. The sun was hot, high in the sky and reflecting off the mirror-like surface of the sea. The boat drew a trail across the water and put Christos in mind of Ariadne's thread in the labyrinth at the Palace of Knossos. But unlike in that legend, he sensed he would never return home.

Michalis harboured his own thoughts. Had he been wrong to leave with his family rather than remain and fight for the girl he loved?

'I'm sorry, Grandad,' Michalis blurted out.

Christos could see a tear in the young man's eye and looked quizzically at his grandson.

'This is all my fault.'

'What are you talking about? We all know it was Tassos who started the blaze.'

'But I provoked him. Has Dad not said anything?'

'Your father has said nothing to me. I don't know what you mean.'

Sitting together as the boat made a steady course west, the regular beat of the engine the only accompaniment to their conversation, Michalis unburdened himself of the guilt he felt over his affair with Sofia.

'You cannot be blamed for loving a woman,' said Christos. 'It's not your fault. Tassos has always been angry, ever since the war. I should have realised it was only a matter of time before he sought retribution, but he has been cleverer than I thought.'

Christos paused, then continued. 'I'm sorry Michali, maybe I should have told you this before. As you know, during the Second World War and the German occupation, I was an *andarte*, a freedom fighter. The Nazis executed as many of the villagers they could find in retribution for our acts of resistance – including Tassos' parents. He has never forgiven me.'

Michalis sat transfixed as his grandfather told him the story. Tassos, still a young boy then, had been taken to a village higher up in the mountains to be looked after by an aunt and uncle. After the war, they moved to the smallholding he had inherited on his parents' death, and worked hard to restore it. The goats which grazed on the scrubby hillside and chickens that scratched around the vegetable patch and beneath the few olive trees made them a meagre living but when his aunt died and his uncle became too old to manage the farm, it began to go to wrack and ruin. Tassos had little inclination to work the land and began to sell the chickens and goats rather than have to collect eggs or do the milking and make cheese. When his uncle passed away, Tassos did the bare minimum. The money from his arranged marriage to Dimitra had given him some respite.

Meanwhile, in the years following the war, Christos and Panagiotis had worked carefully on their vineyard and made a successful business, and it was a thorn in Tassos' side. With the last of his wife's dowry he hired help to clear his land and bought vines to fill the plot. But he had been too lazy to emulate their own neat rows of trimmed vines. Unlike Christos, who produced his own wine, Tassos sent his grapes to the cooperative to be processed. He overplanted the land in the hope of producing a larger crop but his greed and neglect of the vines meant his harvest declined each year. Christos' successful vineyard became a constant reminder of his own shortcomings.

'Burning our vineyard has not only satisfied his need for revenge. He knew that his fascist friends would jump at the excuse of the fire to throw us in jail. Say no more about this nonsense of you being responsible. Your father has said nothing, and it should never be spoken of again.' Christos hugged his grandson, and could feel the tension drain from Michalis' body.

*

It took just twenty minutes for the small ferry to make its way along the coast in the shadow of the stark mountains before turning into a semicircular bay, past a tiny island and a small lighthouse.

To Dimitra, it seemed nothing had changed, though she had not been to Loutro since her wedding to Tassos eighteen years earlier. The arms of the coastline wrapped around the deep blue glass of the waters, disturbed only by the bow wave as they edged towards the jetty. Behind the tiny pebble beach sat a cluster of houses, their white and blue faces turned towards the sparkling sea.

She smiled nervously at Sofia as they disembarked. Quickly she found the way to Despina's door. How unlike the sad life she had led with Tassos was the happy home into which she and her daughter were now welcomed with a deep embrace.

Dimitra and Despina both cried at their reunion. Sofia was smothered in hugs and kisses by her aunt who had never met her before. She felt loved in an easy way she had not 'til that moment experienced. Her three young cousins rushed indoors, dizzy with excitement at meeting them. More tears were shed when Dimitra told her sister of the abuse she had suffered at the hands of her husband.

'You are safe,' Despina reassured her sister and niece. 'He won't dare come here. If he does, when word gets out about how you've been treated, he will be made to pay for his actions, you can count on that. There's no way he can get into the village without us knowing. If he has the nerve to follow you here, my husband Athanasios and his friends will deal with him.'

Dimitra was certain Despina was right, that her cowardly husband would not dare follow them, even if he was so inclined, to this remote south-western corner of the island. The Sfakiots were fiercely independent and protective of their own people and any supporter of the Junta who encroached there would be in jeopardy.

*

A police car drew up at the burned-out vineyard. There was no sign of life, hardly surprising as the roofs of both the house and the winery buildings had collapsed in on the charred remains of all that had lain beneath them. Once-white walls were blackened with smoke and the glass of hundreds of bottles shattered in the inferno littered the courtyard.

The two policemen looked up the mountainside at the scorched earth where once neat rows of vines had stretched. The temperature was already rising, and they had seen enough. Their information from the neighbour was that the fire had been started by negligence or possibly for insurance purposes, and the landowners had fled, an admission of their guilt. They would check in the village to see if anyone knew about the fire or the whereabouts of the family, but they were not optimistic about getting anything.

In the streets of Epano Elounda, none of the villagers they could find to talk to had seen or heard anything of their neighbours for several days, apparently. There was little they could do; the family had left. They would report it to the secret police, who of course would want to pursue and punish anyone whose sympathies did not lie with the Junta. The two officers returned to the coast.

From the chair beside the door of his house, Tassos watched the police car wind its way down the hillside towards Elounda, congratulating himself. Everything had gone to plan. The previous morning, he had disconnected the irrigation pipes on his land, soaking the lower section of his plot with water down to the wall, the other side of which was a break which Christos had left, obsessed by neatness and maybe to stop fire spreading. Tassos had timed setting alight the tinder-dry land almost to perfection. He knew the timing of the afternoon breeze which he hoped would fan the flames up the mountain before easing, stopping and changing direction again.

It had been easy for him to persuade the local authorities not to respond to any calls for firefighters. They hated the villagers who were a continual thorn in their side, and the opportunity to throw a few in jail would look good to their superiors. Tassos had correctly predicted that Christos would flee with his family for fear of arrest, leaving the land for him to grab.

Tassos took another sip of raki. He would be patient. There was no point in rushing these things and anyway, it would take some time for the ground to settle. In the meantime, he would relish the moment. His money worries would soon be over and the neighbours he loathed were gone. He felt a smile creep across his lips, and for the first time in years thought that he might be happy.

Chapter 3

AS THE AFTERNOON drifted into dusk, Christos dozed in the warmth of the cockpit. Petros instructed Panagiotis and Michalis over their watch-keeping duties. If they saw any other vessels they were to get him to take the wheel at any time of day or night. As the flaming sun sank beneath the sea on the distant horizon, the full moon took up the watch, lighting their way towards the Cape of Gramvousa.

Until they took on new supplies, rations were limited; there were some rusks and oil in the cupboard, eggs, tomatoes and hard cheese in the ice box. While Michalis held a steady course, Petros and Panagiotis unwound and baited two lines of hooks, playing them out behind the caique. Half an hour later, pulling them in, the silver, green and olive skins of mackerel glinted in the moonlight and the fish were passed below to Calliope in the small galley.

Pan-fried on the hob in oil with salt and pepper, plates of the fresh fish accompanied by a cheese omelette and dakos were handed up the companionway. After a day at sea, the food could not have tasted better, nor the deep red wine which Petros poured from a large plastic flagon to accompany the feast.

Petros checked the log, calculating they would be making their rendezvous at around six in the morning. It was agreed that Michalis would take the first watch until midnight when Panagiotis would helm through the night until four, then Petros would take over.

The night was uneventful and as it approached six o'clock Petros could make out the white, green and red navigation lights of a vessel coming towards them. He slowed the engine and reached for the handheld microphone of the two-way radio, signalling the boat ahead to confirm it was his friend's caique.

On the calm sea in the first light of dawn, the manoeuvre was easy for the two skippers who brought their vessels together, rafting up side by side. Quickly the cans of fuel were passed between the boats and stowed below, followed by storage boxes of food and drink. In less than half an hour the boats were cast off and drifted apart before Petros swung the helm and set a course north.

By late morning the island of Antikythera came on the horizon, remaining a tiny speck to starboard as they left the Sea of Crete behind. While the caique made its steady progress away from their home, the regular beat of the engine was the only accompaniment to their thoughts.

The upheaval to their lives was still almost too enormous for any of them to contemplate what the future might hold. In Italy they would need to throw themselves on the mercy of the authorities, but they were optimistic they would be accepted as Italy had already given refuge to many escaping the tyranny of the Junta. Everything they owned had been destroyed in the fire and each of them knew that to build a new life they would need to start from nothing.

As the boat sailed onwards, they had mainland Greece and the Ionian archipelago – Zakynthos, Kefalonia, Ithaca, Lefkas – to the east. At night they could see the lights from small villages dotted on the hillsides and from fishing boats casting or hauling their nets inshore.

Christos and Panagiotis sat together in the wheelhouse. As they talked, the older man tried to bolster his son's confidence about the hurdles which lay ahead. He had skills working on the land and in winemaking and business, and was not frightened of hard work. He was sure that between them they would find something to sustain them until their future became clearer. They pooled the drachma they had in their wallets and wondered how many Italian lira that would buy them. Seeing them counting their money, Petros went below, lifting a hatch to the bilges and taking out a metal box.

'Here, have this. I have little need of it. I only keep it hidden to stop the tax man getting his grubby hands on it. Your need is greater than mine. We stood together against the Nazis and we stand together now against those bastards who have destroyed our country.'

Christos opened the lid and took out a wad of notes. He knew his old comrade would accept no argument, and that the money would come in handy, at least until they could find some work in Italy.

'Thank you, Petro, I will be forever indebted to you. Some day I hope I will be able to repay you.'

'It is nothing more than you would do for me,' replied Petros and he turned and took the wheel from Christos, and looked straight ahead out to sea.

Far in the distance they could make out Corfu, the north-westerly border of Greece. Petros turned the boat away from the island. 'In about two and a half hours we should be clear of Greek waters.' As the last vestiges of land sank over the horizon, Christos felt a wave of sadness wash over him. He realised that this might be his last glimpse of the country he loved.

South of the strait of Otranto, where the Ionian and Adriatic Seas met, they held a course towards Salento in Puglia on the heel of Italy. That morning Petros informed them that they had now left Greek territorial waters. They were free. Christos felt relief that they had escaped the clutches of the Junta. In his heart he knew that it had been the only option to keep his family safe.

Through the day they kept a steady speed towards Italy, keeping a watch on the huge ships which crossed their bow, heading south towards Africa or north to Italy or the Balkan ports. The channel was busy with shipping, but it was a clear day and as darkness fell the reassuring flicker of the radar screen made them aware of any approaching vessels. During the night, even if he was not at the helm, Petros did not sleep, preferring to keep a careful eye out for the navigation lights of ships which passed as shadows through the darkness.

The mood was buoyant the following morning as Petros told them they should make landfall in Italy in less than five hours.

They still had a few hours to go when they felt the regular thudding of the engine increase. Christos and Panagiotis both looked enquiringly at Petros at the wheel, his hand on the throttle control. The reassuring rhythm of the engine was replaced by a more urgent juddering as the boat strained to pick up speed. Both men followed Petros' gaze as he looked astern at the empty horizon before glancing back at the radar. Studying the screen they could see a dot travelling in the same direction as the caique at high speed.

'We are being followed,' Petros answered their unasked question. 'They're about fifteen miles away, but the speed they're travelling, they will be upon us in less than an hour.'

'How far are we from land?' Christos asked.

'About seventeen miles, but even at full speed they'll still catch us.' Petros paused and then told Panagiotis to take the helm. 'Hold this course and speed.' The skipper then descended into the cabin.

From below, they could hear him speaking English into the radio. As they scanned the horizon astern, the vibrating of the engine added to their increasing anxiety. At last, Petros emerged.

'I've radioed the Italian coastguard. If we can get within twelve miles of land we will be in their territorial waters and we have a chance. We may be starting an international incident,' he laughed. 'And if we make it, I might have to stay in Italy a bit longer than I intended.'

Christos could see on his friend's face an expression he remembered from the war, a determination in his steely brown eyes and a slight upward turn of his mouth.

Petros handed Christos a pair of binoculars. 'You keep watch. Are you OK on the helm for the moment, Panagioti?' He didn't await a reply but disappeared again down into the cabin. Minutes later he was back carrying a Lee-Enfield rifle, which Christos recognised, clean and oiled. 'I keep this on board just in case.'

Christos could see the glint in his friend's eyes as he loaded the magazine. Concerned for the safety of his family, Christos did not relish the potential confrontation as much as his old comrade. Maria and Calliope in the cockpit were blissfully unaware of the danger they might be facing. He scanned the horizon: still no sign of the chasing vessel.

Petros saw the dot on the horizon first. Holding out a hand, he took the binoculars from his friend. 'They are less than three miles away now. They'll be on us in about quarter of an hour.'

Christos quickly went astern to tell his wife and daughter-in-law and usher them down into the cabin below. Panagiotis willed the caique to go faster, but it was no match for the gunboat, its grey hull now clearly visible behind the white bow wave it threw up as it ploughed towards them.

The radio crackled and Petros swung himself down to the cabin. From the wheelhouse they could make out raised voices as Petros tuned in the channel to hear more clearly. Climbing the stairs again he took the binoculars from Christos and turned them on the boat that was now within a mile of them. It came down off its bow wave and slowed. Turning his gaze ahead, Petros could now make out another vessel coming towards them, closing fast. Reverting his look astern, he saw the Greek navy gunboat turn and speed off in the direction from which it had come.

Christos thought he could see a look of slight disappointment on his friend's face as he picked up the rifle and threw it overboard.

'We don't want any problems with customs.' Petros laughed. 'That was close.' He returned below and, picking up the handset, called the Italian coastguard vessel which was approaching. After checking they were safe, the captain told them to continue towards land while he shadowed the Greek gunboat until it had left Italian waters. He would then return to escort them, ensuring safe passage to shore.

Within half an hour the fast, grey coastguard boat had returned, slowing to fall in ahead of the caique. Petros took the helm and throttled back to a comfortable cruising speed. From afar they could make out the towering lighthouse of Santa Maria di Leuca on the eastern cape of the Gulf of Taranto, and Petros could hear the coastguard on the radio requesting permission from the port to bring the boat to shore.

*

The two women were welcomed into Despina and Athanasios' home in Loutro, along with their three children, and that had been the start of their new life. But the house was crowded and it was a relief to everyone when Despina suggested that Dimitra and her daughter move into their late father's house nearby, their childhood home, which had lain empty since his death two years earlier.

The house was dusty and the paint flaking, but with the shutters thrown open it was light and welcoming, and Dimitra and Sofia set about cleaning and painting the small cottage, turning it into a home. They loved working together and catching the ferry to and from Chora Sfakion to pick up supplies of paint and cleaning materials. For Sofia it was a new start; for Dimitra it was an emotional time, bringing back memories of a former life.

Dimitra gradually realised she was free from the monster who had made her life unbearable. Whether he was scared of the repercussions from her Sfakiot family or whether he was too lazy, it didn't matter. As the days, weeks and months went past she felt more and more secure and gained in confidence. Not wanting to be a burden to her sister's family, she took any opportunity to contribute. That first autumn, Dimitra and Sofia left the village for the long walk up to the steep mountainside olive grove to help Athanasios and Despina with the harvest. The family stayed together in a mountain shack until the crop had been bagged and brought down to the village press.

When the weather was good, Sofia loved to join her uncle on his small fishing boat. Leaving the tiny harbour, they would sail east along the coast to Glyka Nera beach. Athanasios explained to her that cold fresh water drained down from the towering White Mountains and bubbled up here from under the warm, salty Libyan Sea. Off this pebble beach, in the shadow of the almost vertical cliffs, they would cast their nets, returning in the early hours of the morning to haul in their catch. The fish were then taken to the family taverna in Loutro, ready for the grill.

The living was hand to mouth, but the family was happy. They had oil from the olives, milk, cheese and meat from their flock of goats and sheep, and fish from the sea, and the takings from the taverna provided the small amount of cash they needed.

Both Dimitra and Sofia could see a change in each other as they settled into life in Loutro. As time passed, Sofia saw the years drop away from her mother, and Dimitra watched her daughter blossom into a beautiful young woman. When they had first arrived in Loutro, Sofia had often thought of what might have happened to Michalis but, as the months turned into years, the memory of her young lover began to fade.

Part 2

2013-2015

Chapter 4

SOFIA LOOKED DOWN from the balcony onto the streets of Athens. How many times over the last few years she had witnessed the same scene play out. At one end of the road protesters amassed, many hooded, some wearing crash helmets. In the distance she could see the shields of the riot police who lined up against them.

Back when she was still a girl and hadn't even dreamed of setting foot in the capital, there had been similar confrontations in 1974 against the military Junta. Thankfully, the dictatorship had fallen in the summer of that year, almost three years after she and her mother had settled in Loutro.

There had been good days following its demise; she sighed as she recalled them.

Trade in Despina and Athanasios' taverna in Loutro had always been local, supplemented by occasional passing custom from itinerants; but after the downfall of the Junta, they began to notice tourists arriving on the ferry. Some villagers, seeing an opportunity, rented out rooms for the tourists to stay in, and the isolated village became a destination for visitors seeking to get away from the world.

As the taverna got busier, Despina and Athanasios extended their hours and they hired a chef, Milos, from the village of Sougia, a ferry ride to the west beyond the entrance to the Gorge of Samaria. He worked alongside the family in the restaurant. The young man was good-looking, gentle, kind and ambitious, all the things Sofia's father had never been, and it soon became clear that she was falling in love.

Sofia and Milos had married in 1980. Although life in Loutro was idyllic, the young chef had ambitions to run his own taverna and was drawn to the bright lights of Athens. Those times had been full of promise, with Greece flourishing as a democracy; it was a chance for the country, and for her and her husband, to make a new start.

Following the landslide election of Andreas Papandreou in 1981, a wave of optimism meant business was beginning to boom in the capital, and Sofia and Milos moved to Athens, along with Dimitra. They worked hard, and by the time their son Thanos was born in 1988, had established a thriving business of their own and had rented a flat nearby and made it their home.

Thanos had grown up with their taverna and had learned to cook there. It was a job he adored and excelled in and since he had started helping in the kitchen as a young man, he had dreamed of taking over the restaurant. She thought of all the hard work they had put in over the years to build up the business. The taverna had thrived, had been a great success.

But that world had come crashing down. The crisis that had rocked the West's financial institutions had sunk the Greek economy, which it appeared had been built around disguised and unsustainable debt. With the country's foreign creditors circling like vultures, taxes had been hiked and pensions slashed. Mass unemployment had taken hold and the country had fallen into a recession so deep that few could imagine how they could dig themselves out of it.

Now, in the September of 2013, democracy was under threat and there was a resurgence of the far right in the shape of the Golden Dawn party, whose fascist beliefs the demonstrators lined up to oppose. She knew that Thanos was out there with them. She was proud of her son but feared for his safety on the streets.

Milos was at their taverna, and she was alone in the flat. She felt tired; tired of the fighting, tired of all the struggling to make ends meet. She rubbed her eyes before feeling the contours of her aging face with her hands. Where had all the years gone? She heard the smashing of the first petrol bombs and smelled the sting of tear gas in the air. She retreated inside, closing the shutters and locking the windows.

Slipping the bolts, she was taken back to the day more than forty years earlier when her father had imprisoned her; the day which precipitated the events which had eventually brought her here. Since then she had had a good life. But now this... She did not know how she was going to tell Thanos.

With the recent years of austerity, Sofia and Milos had tried to balance the books, but it was no good, they would have to cut and run. The taxes and lease on the taverna had for some time been exceeding their profit and, although they had money put aside for their retirement, to continue running the business would soon erode their savings. She could not allow her family to become destitute. But she felt sick at the thought of having to tell Thanos that they had to close the restaurant and that his own aspirations to be head chef there would be shattered.

Through the shuttered windows of the Athens apartment, Sofia listened to the now familiar sounds of fire-bombs exploding, people shouting and car horns blazing as the pitched battle between protestors and police raged. She worried for her son, who she knew would be in the thick of the action.

Sofia thought too of her mother, who had died six years earlier and had risked everything for her. Dimitra had been so proud of her grandson; she doted on him and he on her. Sofia was proud of Thanos and his ambition to work hard and learn and to follow in his father's footsteps. If anything, he aspired to greater heights with his cooking, although he showed little interest in the nitty-gritty of the business side. That would come, she had thought; but now with the taverna failing and its closure imminent, he would have to find another way in the world.

A tear came to Sofia's eye. Had all their hard work been for nothing? Nearing her sixtieth birthday, she did not have the energy to start another business, even if that had been possible in the economic climate.

Outside it was growing dark and the noise of the riot was getting louder. She steeled herself to open the shutters and again step out onto the balcony. Below, the demonstrators were retreating in the face of a barrage of tear gas. Along the street, parked cars were ablaze as Molotov cocktails were hurled from the shelter of doorways. She heard the door to the apartment open and slam. She turned to see her son, his face smeared with soot, standing by the balcony doors and fell crying into his arms.

'Don't worry, Mama, I'm fine. There's no need to be so upset.' Thanos hugged his mother tightly. For minutes he could not console her.

Sofia smelled the smoke and tear gas on her son, and could not control the tears which soaked his t-shirt. What sort of a world was it they were living in, and how had they not been able to provide better for him? 'I'm so sorry, Thano. I have let you down.'

'What is it, Mama? You could never let me down. It's only a demonstration. Things look much worse than they really are. If it upsets you so much, I promise not to go again.'

'It's not the demonstration, Thano. It's more than that. Your father and I have decided we have to close the business,' she blurted. She had wanted to wait until Milos returned before telling him, but sadness and anger overtook her. 'If not, we will lose everything.'

For a moment Thanos was silent, trying to absorb the news. He had known that things had been difficult for a while but had not thought it would come to this. 'Is that all? That's not the end of the world.' Sofia could see the disappointment in her son's face, despite his attempts to disguise it. He pulled her close again. 'Between us we will survive this. As a family.'

It was late by the time Milos returned. His eyes itched from the miasma of the riot which still hung in the air. He was surprised to learn that Sofia had broken the news already to Thanos, but deep down relieved that their secret was out and that his son appeared reconciled with their decision.

*

Over the following days the reality of the news sank in for Thanos. He walked the streets of Athens and bought newspapers seeking a job as a chef, but no one was hiring. His parents were busy winding up the business, which they had been unable to sell as a going concern. They were struggling to squeeze whatever money they could out of the sale of equipment, fixtures and fittings, but the money they made was paltry.

Sofia could see her husband was anxious. During the day when he was not trying to sell what he could from the taverna, he pored over accounts. At night she could feel him tossing and turning in bed, unable to sleep. She worried for both her husband and son as they tried to plot a course for the future.

'I'm sorry, Sofia. But I don't think we can stay here,' announced Milos to his wife one morning. 'The cost of the rent on the apartment is just too expensive now that we're not working, and even with the little I've managed to get for the stuff from the restaurant, our savings won't last long into our retirement.'

Sofia felt a surprising sense of relief at the news. Ever since she had known that the business would need to close, something in her had wanted them to escape from the capital. Without the work, there was nothing to keep them in the city which seethed now with resentment, violence and despair.

In quieter moments she often looked back fondly to the time she had spent as a young woman on Crete after she and her mother had escaped from the horror of living with her tyrannical father. Perhaps now was the time to return to a more tranquil life; on the island their savings might go further, and maybe Thanos, if he chose to move, could find work. When she broached the idea of going back to the island with Milos, she could tell from the smile on her husband's face that he welcomed the idea of returning.

Every week, Sofia still made a phone call to her aunt in Loutro. For months, Despina had sensed a sadness in her niece; she had not wanted to say anything for fear of prying but had been aware something was amiss. It came as no shock when Sofia announced that they had had to close the business, but when she mooted the idea that her family might return to Loutro, Despina could barely conceal her enthusiasm.

In her early seventies, Despina was still working in the taverna, cooking fish on the outdoor charcoal grill for the lunchtime service. Although rentals on her father's house had slowed with the recession, tourists were coming back and day trippers kept trade ticking over at the taverna. Her husband and their children still made a living from the sea and the land, and the remoteness of the village made their relationship with the taxman somewhat more informal than it might be elsewhere. Having Sofia and her family back would be a breath of fresh air in the small community, and as she and Athanasios got older they could always do with a helping hand with their various endeavours.

It was agreed that Sofia and her family would move back into her grandfather's old house. They would not need to pay any rent. Food and drink was plentiful from the land and sea, and with the simple lifestyle, their savings would go further.

For Sofia, the knowledge that their future was more secure came as a comfort and she looked forward to returning to the place which held such happy memories. But somewhere there lurked another, darker recollection; that of her father and his mistreatment of her and her late mother. She had heard no news of him since the day she had escaped the village. She returned the thought to the back of her mind. If her father was still alive he would be nearly eighty and could do no harm to her at the other end of the island where they would be living amongst family.

After struggling to keep the taverna afloat, Milos realised that a weight had been lifted off his shoulders, and for the first time in several years he was feeling optimistic.

It took Thanos some time to come round to the idea. At first, he was unnerved that the future which he thought had been mapped out for him had now disappeared. But he had never been to Crete and as the days went by, he began to think of the move as an adventure.

Once the decision was made that they would move back to Loutro, the days were spent packing up possessions and saying goodbyes. Sofia was not as sad as she expected to be when they closed the door on the Athens apartment for the last time. Tears came to her eyes, but as her husband put a comforting arm around her, she realised they were not tears of sadness but of relief. At last they were escaping the torment of the last few years of struggling to keep their lives afloat. She looked at her son who gave her a reassuring smile, picked up her bag and led his parents down to the waiting taxi.

They boarded the ferry at Piraeus and found seats on deck. Sofia remembered the day she had first arrived in Loutro, and then later in Athens, newly married and full of hope. Her mother had been alive then and she had been so elated about what lay ahead. She had so many good memories, how could she be unhappy with the hand life had dealt her? She looked at Milos, still handsome, caring and kind. If he had lost some of the ambition of his youth, so much the better as they sought more peace in their old age. And Thanos, the son they had brought into the world together, was now a man. She saw her son smile, his tall wiry frame reminiscent of his father when he was younger. Her heart swelled with pride. As the sun got lower, the crew cast off the lines from the dock. In that moment, she put aside any worries she had about the future.

As dusk fell, many of the late-season tourists went below to the restaurants and bars. Sofia and her family remained on deck, watching as the lights of the capital came on and receded into the distance, eventually becoming just a glow on the horizon. The ferry stirred the surface of the water as it pushed purposefully forward into the slight swell. A priest in his stovepipe hat gazed out to sea and an elderly woman dressed in black put a cage with a clucking chicken beneath a bench as she busied herself preparing a makeshift bed on deck.

The night was balmy, the heat tempered by the breeze as the ship made headway south. Occasionally the lights of distant islands would appear like ghostly cruise liners at anchor on the horizon. In the early hours, a chill descended, hanging damp above the deck. Milos reached into a bag, taking out a cardigan which he wrapped around his wife's shoulders. She looked at her son, his eyes closed as he sat on a bench, and smiled at her husband. Throughout the night, she tried to catch some sleep but was too on edge to settle. Despite the cool of the night air, Milos had a warm feeling inside about returning home to Crete which surprised him.

*

A wild bouquet garni of thyme, sage and parched earth drifted in on the breeze which ushered in daybreak and Sofia felt her heart lift as she saw Crete emerge from the misty dawn. As the ship drew closer to land, she could make out the solid walls of the Venetian fortress which stood sentinel, protecting the old harbour as they slipped past towards the port of Heraklion.

The hawsers dropped to the quay, the vessel was winched towards shore and the crowd of friends, family and hawkers waiting to welcome the ship. They looked down from the rail and spotted Despina and Athanasios standing apart from the crowd. Sofia waved but could not attract their attention. The family hurried to disembark, and her aunt and uncle recognised them as they approached.

Despite the years since they had seen each other in the flesh, Sofia was amazed at how kind time had been to Despina and Athanasios. Both in their seventies, they looked much younger. Despina was short and lithe, her face framed by her bobbed, slightly greying hair; Athanasios tall, his body muscular and tanned from a life working on the land and out at sea on his boat. They hugged each other before Athanasios led them to where he had parked his large truck.

Despina insisted on sitting in the back between Sofia and Thanos, with Milos in the front alongside her husband. As they left the city behind, and the truck climbed into the olive-cloaked mountains, Sofia's eyes filled with tears at the recollection of her escape by bus along this very route forty years before when she had been little more than a girl. Despina sensed her melancholy and grasped her hand.

'I'm sorry, Despina. I didn't mean to cry. I'm really happy to be back on Crete. There are just so many emotions and memories of mother and I'm a bit tired from the journey.'

They pulled over at a garage and after filling up with diesel bought some snacks to eat in the car. While the others ate the pastries ravenously, Sofia only nibbled at hers.

'Try and rest, we've a long way to go,' said Despina, squeezing her arm.

Sofia found herself fighting with her eyes, eventually as the sun rose in the sky and the day grew warmer, she succumbed to tiredness. By the time Athanasios turned off the main highway into the White Mountains, she was sound asleep.

Thanos was wide awake, however. He drank in the remote landscape as they crossed the foothills of the mountain range before dropping down, the road twisting and turning as it made its way towards the bluest of seas which glimmered in the distance. How different this was from the hustle of the Athens streets where he had grown up. Already he felt more relaxed than he could remember.

Sofia opened her eyes as the truck pulled up on the quayside in Chora Sfakion. She remembered the small blue ferry moored on the jetty as the same boat which she had taken so many times when she had lived here with her mother.

Athanasios unloaded their luggage onto the dock. He would drive the truck up the mountain tracks to his land above Loutro before walking the paths down to village. The others would take the short journey along the coast. They were lucky: the ferry was due to depart in twenty minutes. The crew stowed their luggage before taking Sofia's hand to help her step aboard. As his mother settled with Despina into seats at the aft of the boat, Thanos stood at the rails taking in everything around him. He felt his father's arm around his shoulders. 'I'd forgotten how beautiful it is here,' Milos said quietly as the lines were cast off from the quay.

Leaving the harbour behind, the ferry headed out to sea before turning westwards and cruising in the shadow of the mountains. Sofia felt her heart lift as she saw the small bay of Glyka Nera. She stood up to join Thanos and told him how she used to go there with Athanasios on his fishing boat, and that the name, 'sweet water', referred to the cold, fresh water which drained down from the mountains and welled up on the sands and beneath the seabed. At one end of the pebble beach a row of tamarisk trees grew beneath the dark brown cliffs, at the other stood a taverna, which Despina told them served the needs of the tourists who came by boat or walking the hillside paths from Chora Sfakion or Loutro to swim.

Leaving the beach behind, they soon entered the semicircular bay of Loutro, passing the tiny island with its small lighthouse. It was just as Sofia had remembered it, the sunshine reflecting off the white houses which overlooked the gin-clear water as the boat edged towards the jetty.

After unloading their luggage from the ferry, it was only a few steps to Despina's taverna, and not much further into the maze of alleyways which lay behind before they arrived back at the house Sofia had left to start a new life in Athens all those years ago. Despina opened the door and handed her the key.

'I'll leave you to settle in and freshen up. When you're ready, come to the taverna for some food.' Despina hugged her niece tight, kissing her on the cheek. 'It's so good to have you back,' she whispered.

When her aunt left, Sofia, Milos and Thanos looked round the house. It was clean and welcoming, the windows looking out onto the lane outside through which they could smell the sea just a few footsteps from their front door. Sofia looked at her husband. 'It's just as I remember.' Milos took her hand and squeezed it. On the table was a bowl of fruit and some biscuits. The fridge was cold and stocked with water and a few other essentials. The beds had been made up and, had they not been hungry, they could have fallen straight into them. Instead, they made their way to the taverna.

The afternoon air was beginning to cool as they were shown to a table by Despina, who sat down with them on the waterfront terrace, the sea only feet away. The chairs were more comfortable than the ones Sofia remembered, and the once bare tables were now covered with blue and white checked cloths. Other than that, little in the taverna appeared to have changed. Despina called to the waitress, and in no time two carafes of wine, one red, one white, were delivered along with water to the table. It was not long before plates of mezzes began to arrive. Snails fried in salty olive oil, fava, village sausages, egg staka and smoky pork belly, crispy squid, salads and myzithra cheese pies drizzled in thyme and honey. Sitting in the taverna brought back fading memories for Milos too, of the days when he had left his home to work here as a chef and had first met his wife.

Sofia looked out to sea. In the distance a ship ploughed its way towards the horizon heading for Africa. For a moment she closed her eyes and a wave of contentment at being back on the island of her birth washed over her. For the first time in months, she felt relaxed. Looking at her husband, the afternoon sun on his face appeared to have stripped away the years, and her son looked more cheerful than she had seen him for some time. Living in her grandparents' house and with the small amount of money they had saved, if they were frugal, they could be happy. Across the table Milos and Thanos ate hungrily, her son asking his father to tell him the recipes for the local dishes he had cooked when he worked here as a young man.

Looking around at the mountains and the sea, there was something about the food which caught Thanos' imagination. It was unlike the dishes they had created in the taverna in Athens which nodded towards the cuisine of Europe. The food they were eating here was more authentic. Each mouthful seemed deeply rooted in the land and waters around them and had a heritage which linked the present with a past stretching back thousands of years.

He had felt insecure when he first learned their taverna in Athens was to close. But now he recognised that he had been spared the pressure of running a business in the capital. His temperament would not have suited the relentless need to make the margins required to pay the lease, the large staff and other overheads. He knew he would have been unhappy taking on so much responsibility and, looking back, realised he had only gone along with the idea so as not to disappoint his parents. He loved being a chef, but wanted to cook authentic food using the freshest produce. What's more, although he had only arrived on the island early that morning, he already felt at home.

'This food is beautiful,' Thanos said to Despina across the table.

'Most of it comes from our smallholding up the mountain or from these fishing boats.' She proudly gestured towards the vessels moored where the terrace met the sea and to a few caiques anchored in the bay. 'I'm pleased you like our food. Your mother has told me what a talented chef you have become, so that means a lot to me. Thank you.'

'To me, this food is better than any of the dishes I can cook.' Thanos looked at Sofia and Milos. 'I'm sorry Mama and Baba, the dishes in our taverna were great but it is food like this I would really like to prepare.'

'Then we will teach you,' said Despina, beaming. 'We can always do with help in the kitchen.' She gestured at the tables which had filled up with tourists as they had been eating. 'We can't pay much…'

'I would love to,' Thanos said eagerly. 'Thank you very much, Despina. When can I start?'

Chapter 5

ON THAT FIRST day Thanos was up early, energised by the prospect of his new job. Despina was pleased to see him already outside the taverna when she came to open up. She introduced him to the chef and later to the waiters and he was put to work doing prep in the kitchen. He asked questions about how the kitchen was organised and about the dishes on the menu, which they were happy to answer. When customers arrived, he was keen to help out with the cooking, happy to fry, grill, sauté or put dishes in the clay ovens to slow roast. By the end of the day it was obvious to all that he was an accomplished chef, and they were happy to have him aboard.

In the early mornings he began to join the chef on the quayside to select the best of the catch landed by the local fishermen; different months brought to shore bright-eyed bass and bream, striped mackerel, gleaming red mullet, squid, octopus and the occasional lobster. When not working in the kitchens he would walk in the mountains and forage wild herbs and greens which he took home to experiment with in new dishes, serving them up for his parents to sample. They were impressed, and moved that their son was excited by the flavours they had grown up with.

Milos was pleased not to be working after all the years running his business in Athens, and initially spent his days walking in the hillsides or playing tavli in a local kafenio. Gradually he started to help Athanasios on his land high up in the White Mountains, harvesting vegetables and fruit, herding and milking goats or making cheese. His new life took him back to his boyhood days in Sougia not far to the west. Once in a while, if the sea was calm, Athanasios would take out his boat to fish and Milos would join him, and took pleasure in seeing their catch served up in the taverna later in the day.

As autumn edged into winter and the taverna was less busy, the whole family joined with friends in the hillsides spreading nets beneath the olive trees, using wooden rakes to beat the fruit from the branches ready for bagging. That first year, when the harvest was in, Thanos offered to roast a sheep over an olivewood fire to feed the workers. As darkness fell, a lyra struck up a haunting melody, joined by a guitar, and under the light of the moon in the warmth of the embers from the fire, they ate, drank and danced well into the night.

As the year moved towards its end the days grew quieter. Few visitors came to the village and the taverna opened only at the weekends, catering mostly for the locals. Thanos loved these days. Some were sparkling, the low diamond sun reflecting off the sea and the snow on the White Mountains, while on other days angry waves seethed in the bay and low clouds hid the ghostlike peaks which loomed above.

When Christmas came, the boats in the bay were strung with lights, and the delicious smell of sweet pastry treats hung in the air. At Epiphany they went to Chora Sfakion and Sofia watched with pride as her son joined the other young men diving into the sea for the cross. When the nights were cold and the taverna was closed, they would light a fire in the cottage using olivewood pruned from the grove. On the radio they heard news of the ongoing recession and Sofia took comfort at their decision to retire to the village. Here the family could survive on the little money they had saved and what the land and the sea around them provided. She could not remember a time when she had been so at ease. As she looked at her husband snoozing in his chair and her son happily cooking up a new recipe for them to try for their dinner, she felt content.

At Easter, Thanos and Milos got up early to roast a lamb. As they feasted, Sofia looked forward to the days of summer and relished in the life she had found with her whole family around her. She spent her days looking after their new home, sometimes running errands on the ferry to Chora Sfakion. She loved walking in the mountains and sitting on the beach, reading or staring out to sea.

With the Easter celebrations over, they began to prepare for the first tourists who were starting to arrive on the ferries, some to experience the wonderful seclusion of the village, others stopping off after hiking down the nearby Samaria Gorge. Thanos relished his work at the taverna. The chef was impressed by his recipes and put a couple of the dishes he had developed on the new-season menu: lamb shanks dotted with garlic and rosemary, and boned pork knuckle filled with bay leaves, apple and garlic stuffing, both dishes cooked in the wood-fired oven.

*

Tassos had died at home. He had stumbled while going to the refrigerator to get another karafaki of raki, hitting his head on the corner of a table. His absence from this earth had gone unnoticed for days. Eventually a shepherd who had not spied him sitting outside his door for some time decided to investigate and found him lying dead on the floor. His death was not investigated, there was no autopsy. At Tassos' advanced age it was assumed that he had died of a heart attack.

It was late August when the call came to Despina.

'My name is Georgia Kirmizaki, a solicitor from Agios Nikolaos.' Sofia felt her heart plummet. 'I'm sorry to have to bring you the news that your father died a month ago. Since then I have been trying to trace any relatives.'

Georgia explained that she had found Sofia's name in the civil register at the mayor's office. Research through the official records had led her to Dimitra's birthplace of Loutro, and through her family name to Despina. Tassos had died without a will and through the Greek law of forced heirship, Sofia was the sole beneficiary of his estate.

When Sofia replaced the receiver, all the colour had drained from her. Since she and her mother had sought shelter with Despina in Loutro more than forty years earlier, the story of their lives in Epano Elounda had been mentioned as little as possible. Sofia had confided in Milos before they had married, and he too had thought it best that for the sake of his new wife's health that the events of her childhood were forgotten.

As Thanos grew up and began asking questions about his grandfather, Sofia and Dimitra had told him that he had died – perhaps, she hoped, he had – and her demeanour when the subject was mentioned had not encouraged him to ask further questions. She had long banished the memory of her brutal father from her thoughts in the hope that he had indeed died.

Now confronted with the reality of her father's death, Sofia felt no sorrow for him, but unhappy memories of her childhood and the abuse she and her mother had suffered came flooding to the forefront of her mind. It was impossible to conceal her feelings and the pain washed through her in waves. Milos encircled her in his arms as Thanos looked on, confused and concerned by his mother's distress.

'I think you need to tell him,' Milos whispered in his wife's ear.

It took some time before Sofia could speak. When she had been settled in a chair and brought some water, she began to open up. Thanos sat in silence as his mother revealed the secrets of their family history.

First, she apologised to Thanos: his grandfather, Tassos, had in fact been alive until recently. She was sorry for lying, but it was the only way she could think of to rid herself of the trauma of her past. She hoped he would forgive her when she explained.

She then recalled what her mother had learned from people in their village.

Tassos was still a child during the Second World War and the German occupation of Crete. In Epano Elounda, the villagers had supported the local partisans and foreign Special Forces to show their resistance, though the Nazis were known to be brutal in their reprisals. One night when Tassos was ten, his parents had hidden him in his mother's dowry chest before they were dragged away from their home. Trembling in the darkness he heard the gunfire of the Nazi execution squad and knew his parents had been murdered along with everyone else the soldiers had found in the village. The petrified young Tassos had been discovered still hiding some hours after the death squad had departed.

Christos, who had the neighbouring farm and was known to be an *andarte*, had left the village and taken his family up into the mountains for safety. In Tassos' young mind, those freedom fighters' acts had led to the death of his parents and he would never forgive them. Sofia didn't know all the details, but said her mother had told her that through the civil war that followed, living next door to the people who he blamed for his parents' demise, he became increasingly angry and twisted.

Sofia then told Thanos of her own painful memories, and how she had never been shown any love by her father. He had neglected his family as he had his vines, spending his days drinking raki and shouting at her mother before disappearing down the mountain, only to return late at night raging and violent. Thanos shuddered at the thought of the abuse of his grandmother, the gentle, kind woman who had lived with them when he was growing up in Athens.

Sofia steeled herself to tell her son the story of her relationship with Michalis. She struggled as she told Thanos of the day her father had caught her together with her boyfriend. How he had dragged her back to the house and imprisoned her and how she and her mother had escaped during the fire Tassos had started.

'I'm sorry Thano. I should have told you this before. Now you know the truth.'

Thanos said nothing, but enveloped his mother in a hug.

*

Sofia had not been to eastern Crete since her mother had helped her escape. The thought of being there brought back too many memories of the place where she and her mother had been forced to live in fear. So she was reluctant to attend the meeting Georgia had requested, hoping Sofia might be able to help untangle some complications she had encountered in trying to settle the estate.

'It might let you find closure,' Milos suggested. 'It could help you finally put all this behind you.'

'I'm more than happy to take you in the truck,' Athanasios said. With all the family offering to go with her for moral support, she finally agreed.

It was not yet the end of the tourist season and the taverna was still busy, but Despina set about making arrangements for her staff to manage without them for a couple of days.

It would be a long journey and Thanos suggested that they stay overnight before returning the following morning. But Sofia was adamant she would not stay any longer than she needed to. She wanted to get the meeting over and done with as quickly as possible and get home to Loutro. Eventually, realising Athanasios would be tired and she was being unfair to her uncle and aunt, she agreed that they would stop over in Heraklion on their return.

On the day of the meeting, Sofia struggled to get out of bed. She had found sleeping difficult and felt drained. All she wanted to do was pull the covers over her head and shut out the world. Milos could sense her anxiety and with reassurances and gentle cajoling he managed to get her up and ready for the journey.

Taking the first ferry of the morning to Chora Sfakion, they joined Athanasios with his truck. Milos had offered to do the long drive, but Athanasios had laughed, saying he knew the roads like the back of his hand and that Milos should look after Sofia. Even crossing the foothills of the mountains, the September sun made its intentions for the day felt. By the time they reached the northern coast the heat was stifling. Sofia was drowsy and closed her eyes. Sleeping would make the journey pass more quickly.

Agios Nikolaos had changed so much since the days of her childhood, she thought, now awake as they drove into the city. It had grown so much bigger, and what had once been fields were now shops and supermarkets. The meeting had been set for late afternoon, and Athanasios had timed the journey well. They arrived an hour early, allowing time for a coffee in the main square. The centre was less changed, but the familiarity did little to settle the unease Sofia felt.

*

After the solicitor had checked Sofia's documents to prove her identity she got down to business. Milos held his wife's hand as she was told of how her elderly father had been discovered dead at his home and had been buried in the nearby hillside cemetery some weeks ago. Sofia felt no emotion and sat stony-faced. In some strange way, the facts of his death allowed her to regain some composure. Despite her worries about returning to a place that reminded her of an unhappy childhood, she was empty inside.

Business turned to her father's estate. In monetary terms that amounted to little, some cash which had been found in a tin in the rundown farmhouse. But the house itself and the land now belonged to Sofia. The solicitor needed to transfer the deeds of the property into her name, but had encountered a problem. When she requested details of the property from the land registry to begin the conveyance, she discovered that much of the farm had not legally belonged to Tassos.

'Can I see the plan?' Sofia asked reluctantly. The lawyer slid a sheet of paper across the table. A dotted line delineated the extent of the property which had been thought to belong to her father, but two areas marked in different-coloured ink showed that only half the land was his.

The realisation of what had happened dawned on Sofia and sent her spiralling into memories she had tried for so long to erase. She saw the face of Michalis, and remembered how her father had dragged her home and imprisoned her. She remembered her mother frantically pushing her out the door and urging her up the mountain, and then looking back at the burning hillside. Her mother had told her later that Tassos had started the fire and had seen to it that Michalis' family would have to flee. She had put all this from her mind, trying to forget the consequences of her love for Michalis. If ever she thought about it, she assumed that Michalis and his family had returned to their vineyard after the fall of the military Junta.

'I know who owns the land,' Sofia said. 'I don't want anything to do with it.' Not only had her father's legacy trawled up nightmares, but now she felt guilty that he had stolen land from Michalis' family, which they had seemingly never been able to reclaim. The full extent of what Tassos had done hit her, and all as a reaction to seeing her with Michalis. She began to sweat and thought she was going to be sick.

'I have got the name of the landowner from the land registry but have taken it no further. Do you want me to continue searching? It could take a long time and cost a lot of money, but if you are to inherit your father's land, we need to sort this out.'

Sofia was in turmoil. She wished she had never agreed to meet with the solicitor. Her head was in a fog. She felt an eye twitch involuntarily before her whole body began to shake.

'We should call an ambulance,' Milos said, worry written across his face.

'It would be quicker to drive – the hospital's not far up the road.' Georgia grabbed her bag. 'I'll come with you and show you the way.'

Thanos and his father helped Sofia to stand and make her way outside and into the car. It took only minutes for them to reach the hospital, Milos unable to console his wife who sat distraught beside him on the back seat.

Admitted to the emergency department, with an oxygen mask over her face and connected to a heart monitor, she felt calmer. The doctor explained she had suffered an anxiety attack. She felt a needle in her hand and a nurse took some blood from the cannula she had inserted into a vein.

'If these are OK, you can go. The results will take an hour or two.'

As the nurse left the bedside, Sofia felt a tear roll down her cheek and turned to Milos. 'I'm sorry, I don't think I can deal with this.'

Milos squeezed her hand. 'If it's OK, I can try and look after everything for you.' He glanced at the solicitor who nodded.

'Your wife can either sign a power of attorney, or you can get her to put her name on the relevant papers as and when they turn up. Either way, we will sort it out. We can talk on the phone and decide how you would like to proceed. Give me a ring and let me know. I'd better get back to work.'

'Thank you for all you've done. I'll be in touch,' said Milos as the lawyer turned and left.

It was dark by the time Sofia was discharged from hospital and they got into the truck and headed towards Heraklion. She felt her husband's arm around her shoulder and heard him whisper, 'Don't worry. I'll look after this.'

Chapter 6

MICHALIS SMILED AS he stepped onto the terrace which surrounded the house and felt the warmth of the sunshine on his skin. The short-lived storm was over. He looked up and could see the billowing clouds being blown away on the south-westerly wind. This year's crop looked to be the best since they had planted the vines twenty-two years earlier, the year before Chloe had been born.

Now the daughter he doted on was on her way home from Italy, where she had been working at her grandfather's vineyard, gaining wider experience of the trade she wanted to pursue. Although Panagiotis was eighty years old, he still played an active part in running the business he built from scratch after escaping from Greece. Once she got back, Chloe would be able to help them bring in the plump green acid chardonnay grapes which had thrived on the terroir of their Kentish vineyard. Already their sparkling wines were getting good reviews from the critics, who compared them favourably with Champagne and, although it would take some years for this year's crop to be ready for market, Michalis was certain the wine would be the best they had ever produced.

He felt an arm wrap around his shoulders and, as he turned, Charlotte kissed him on his head. He took her hands and kissed her on the mouth.

'There's no time for that,' his wife said, laughing. 'We have to get to work. The weather looks set fair and the forecast is good for the next few days at least. The workers will be here in half an hour to help with the picking. You'd best bring the tractor and trailer round from the barn.'

Hitching up the trailer, he climbed onto the tractor and, sitting for a moment, thought how far he had come since the day they had lost everything and had to flee Crete. He was now sixty years old and could not have been happier, settled in England. Every year since he had moved to Kent, he and Charlotte visited his father and mother in Puglia. He was proud of what his parents had achieved and, although his grandparents had been dead for some years now, he would be eternally grateful to them for helping the family escape from Crete all those years ago.

As they had hoped, the Italian authorities had granted the family asylum. The money Petros had so generously given them, along with the drachma in their wallets, they had exchanged for enough lira to pay several months' rent on a tumbledown farmhouse. It was not long before the experienced Panagiotis had found work at a local vineyard, and Michalis had soon found a job working alongside his father. The labour was hard and they worked long hours, but they lived frugally and every week Panagiotis managed to put aside some savings.

Three years after the family's arrival in Italy, the debacle of the Turkish invasion of Cyprus led to the overthrow of the military Junta in Greece. Some months later, the family had been able to get passports issued to them via the Greek embassy. Although they were then free to return, Panagiotis had saved enough to put down the deposit on a small plot of land and start his own business in Italy. He saw that the opportunities in the wine trade there were years ahead of the market in Greece, and he knew there would be nothing in Crete for them to return to.

They had made good friends in their Italian village community and Panagiotis was always keen to help his neighbours with his knowledge and labour. Thanks to this, people he knew donated cuttings of vines to plant alongside the initial small stock they bought to establish their vineyard. For the first few years both Panagiotis and Michalis would work for other winemakers in the fields and in their wineries, each year buying and grafting more vines. It would take three years before they could make their first batch of wine and some years more before the volume was enough to turn a profit.

His father had been patient and diligent. He had been careful not to plant his vines too close together but in rows where they would not be scorched by the sun and would be cooled by the prevailing breezes. Although the plot was small, the quality of his father's wine improved with every vintage. With his growing reputation for quality, he was able to charge a good price for the cases of wine which were shipped outside of the region and even abroad. Soon he had been able to buy more land and expand the business.

Every day Michalis could not believe how fortunate he had been to meet Charlotte. With the guilt he had felt about the consequences of his affair with Sofia all those years ago in Crete – despite the reassurances of his grandfather that he had not been to blame – and the isolation of their lives in Italy, Michalis had given up on finding love. He had been over thirty years old when Charlotte came into his life, a young woman some ten years his junior who had arrived from her home in England for a working holiday in Italy to gain experience in the wine-making trade.

Her work experience over, she had returned to England to help on her parents' fledgling vineyard, but came back for holidays and their romance blossomed. Two years after meeting, Michalis had plucked up the courage to propose, and the couple had taken the hard decision that Michalis would move with his young bride to live in England, leaving his parents behind to run their small vineyard which they had worked so hard to establish in Italy. They left with the blessing of his parents and grandparents, who were pleased to see him happy and to at last shed the guilt they knew he felt about the fire which had changed the course of all their lives.

When Charlotte's parents had retired, she and Michalis had taken over the running of the winery. They had moved the business from producing white and red wines for the middle market to establishing a growing reputation for making fine sparkling wines.

Michalis was pleased that his grandparents had lived long enough to see the birth of Chloe and the establishment of both vineyards. Christos and Maria had died peacefully within months of each other. If his grandfather had ever regretted leaving the land whose freedom he had fought so hard for in the war, he had never voiced his thoughts. He was always looking forward, positive and supportive of his family's endeavours.

Michalis heard the minibus pull into the yard and the cheerful voice of Charlotte greeting the agency workers, many of whom returned year after year to help them pick the grapes. He started the engine and drove the tractor from the barn to the first row of vines. He had done a last-minute check on the sugar and acidity levels of the fruit, which were perfect and would need little adjustment in the wine-making process. If the weather stayed warm and sunny for the twelve days he estimated that it would take to bring the harvest in, the grapes should yield a classic vintage.

While the pickers selected their tools, either shears or knives, Michalis drove between the rows of vines putting down the empty plastic crates which they would fill ready for him to collect and transport to the winery. The previous day he had laid out the lights and cables in case the weather deteriorated and they needed to work late into the night. He loved this time of year and always felt animated as the pickers set off down the rows, harvesting the first bunches of fruit. It was a time of optimism. His face lit up even further as he saw Chloe walk through the yard, abandon her suitcase and run towards her mother.

'I made it! I didn't want to miss the start of the harvest. Just give me a moment to change and grab my secateurs. I'll be right with you.'

Michalis got down from the tractor and embraced his daughter. 'I'm sure we can wait a few minutes longer. Go on, get changed. It's great to see you.'

He looked at his wife beaming to have her child home. How much of Charlotte he saw in Chloe; both strong, beautiful women. As he climbed back onto the tractor he thought how fortunate he was to be alive.

*

It was not the first occasion that Georgia had tried to untangle disputes over land. Although it was time-consuming, the lawyer rather enjoyed attempting to trace long-lost relatives so that she could tie up a case. Wading through the bureaucracy could be painstaking, but family trees could usually be unravelled. This search was a complicated one.

Although anecdotal evidence she had gleaned from villagers in Epano Elounda suggested Christos and his family had left the country during the Junta years, nothing of their clandestine escape had been recorded. She struck lucky when she found the certificate of his son Panagiotis' wedding to Calliope at the municipality registration office. From this she noted Calliope's maiden name and that she came from Kritsa, a village not far from Agios Nikolaos. Cross-checking the surname against the register of births, she found several people of the same name in the village. Visiting, she made enquiries and it did not take long to discover Calliope had a surviving sister, still living in Kritsa.

At first the woman was suspicious, but Georgia eventually gained her trust and learned that she was still in contact with Calliope. She agreed to ask her sister to get Panagiotis to contact the lawyer.

*

The weather was kind, and with only one day lost to rain, the harvest was completed within a fortnight. As the last trailer-load was emptied into the press, Michalis could see the sun setting through the open door of the winery. He turned the tap and filled a glass with the fresh grape juice. Minutes before, the bunches had been on the vine; now he hoped to confirm from the juice that this would be a vintage year. As he put the glass to his lips, he felt his phone vibrate in his pocket.

'Hi Dad! You caught me just as I was about to have a first taste. Everything OK?'

Panagiotis had at first hesitated to phone his son. The call from the lawyer in Crete had brought back unwelcome recollections of the past, of the vineyard and home they had lost in the fire. What use was that land to them now? He had discussed it with Calliope, and they both agreed they did not want to be burdened with it – or the paperwork involved – at their age. But Michalis had the right to the option of having the property passed on to him. He was worried, though, that news of the old vineyard in Epano Elounda might bring back the feelings of guilt that Michalis had when he was younger.

'Something from the past has reared its head,' said Panagiotis, and he explained what had happened. He said they had a choice: to reclaim the land or sign it over to Tassos' estate. 'Think about it, and ring me back later if you have time.'

Michalis put down the glass, surprised to find himself unsteady on his feet. The news did indeed bring back unwanted memories. He had no desire to think about the village of his childhood where so much had been lost. Michalis had always been open with Charlotte about what had caused his family's flight from Crete. But the sad circumstances meant that they had been reluctant to pass down the details to Chloe. All they had revealed to her was that her father and grandparents had left the country to get away from the fascist dictatorship. She had not questioned this or asked for any details, so they had been content to let the matter rest.

Putting the phone back in his pocket, Michalis took a bottle from the huge rack in the cellar next to the winery and walked across the courtyard to the house, opening the door into the kitchen where his wife and daughter sat deep in conversation at the table drinking tea.

'Here, I think we all could do with something stronger.' Michalis took the bottle to the fridge, replacing the chilled one he now placed on the table before taking three glasses from a cupboard. Removing the foil, he loosened the muselet from the cork, before popping it out and pouring.

'To the vintage of 2014.' Michalis raised his glass.

'I'll drink to that,' said Charlotte, clinking her glass on her husband's.

'Cheers,' said Chloe yawning. 'I'm exhausted. We deserve this.'

Michalis saw his wife and daughter smiling at him. How happy they were and how good life was, so why had his contentment been interrupted by a reminder of the past?

He hesitated. 'I've just had my dad on the phone.'

'How is he?' asked Chloe.

'He's fine. But he had some news.' Michalis turned and looked at Charlotte. 'It's about the vineyard in Crete.'

'What vineyard in Crete?' Chloe looked enquiringly at her father.

Charlotte grabbed hold of her husband's hand beneath the table and nodded. He took a breath and embarked on telling the story of why they had been forced to flee the Junta in fear of their lives.

'Let's see, it goes all the way back to the end of the Second World War. My grandfather, your great-grandfather Christos, had been a freedom fighter in the resistance against the Nazis.'

'Wow, really?' said Chloe, wide-eyed.

'Yes. It's a bit of a long story,' he said apologetically, topping up all their glasses, and then continued.

'To most people, *andartes* like your great-grandfather were heroes. But the people who had the adjacent land were murdered by the Nazi death squads in retribution, along with other villagers, and their young son, Tassos, never forgave our family, who he blamed for the loss of his parents.'

Michalis explained how the flames of Tassos' anger had been fanned over the years by the success of their own family's vineyard, which he had tried to emulate, but with no inclination to work hard. He had greedily planted too many vines in the vain hope of a bumper crop. Over the years his neglected land became less and less productive and he became more hostile.

Michalis looked down and paused, fiddling with the stem of his wine glass. He took a deep breath and resumed the story. 'The final straw was when I became romantically involved with Tassos' daughter, Sofia, and his resentment finally boiled over when he saw us kissing. His revenge was calculated and swift, setting fire to our property, destroying our home and livelihood. What's more, because our family was against the Junta, we were blamed for illegally starting a wildfire and were forced to flee to avoid certain arrest. It seems that Tassos then took over my grandfather's land, but now Tassos has died and the lawyer tracked us down as the legal owners. That's what your grandfather called to tell me.'

Michalis sighed, relieved to have the whole story out in the open. Strangely, he thought, looking at his daughter's face for her reaction, Chloe seemed interested but unperturbed to hear about it all, and now he wished he had told her before.

'If all this hadn't happened, Dad, you wouldn't have met Mum, and I wouldn't be here.' Chloe laughed. 'So, what are you going to do about your land?'

'Well, it's not my land, it's your grandfather's, but he wants to discuss it later. He has already told me he doesn't want it and he's not moving from Italy. I don't want it either – we're happy and settled here, and have our hands full, and it wouldn't make sense to manage it long-distance. But one way or another we have to do something. We at least need to register the land which I presume will still be in my grandfather's name.'

Chapter 7

OVER THE FOLLOWING days, Michalis and his father spent hours on the phone discussing the land. Panagiotis was adamant that he wanted nothing to do with it and Michalis was also content with his life in England and not keen to take on the responsibility. They decided the sensible thing to do would be to sell the plot. To do that they would need to go to Crete in person to show evidence of Christos' death and of Panagiotis' identity and right to inherit under the forced heirship laws. They would have to return to Crete if this shadow from the past was not to hang over them.

Their procrastination was brought to an end by Chloe. The story of her family past had awakened in her a curiosity to find out more about the island. After all, she was half Greek, and although since she was a child her father had encouraged her to speak the language, she had never visited the country of her ancestry. She offered to travel with her father and grandfather to Crete, and her enthusiasm persuaded Michalis and Panagiotis to bite the bullet.

Charlotte was happy that her husband was at last confronting an issue which she had always felt had lingered deep inside him; she also agreed that it would do Chloe good to find a connection with her Greek heritage. Charlotte was content to stay at home and look after the family business while her husband and daughter went away for a week to Crete, travelling first to Italy so they could escort the elderly Panagiotis to the island.

It was agreed that they would meet Panagiotis in Brindisi, then take an overnight ferry to Corfu. From there they would catch a morning flight stopping over in Athens to Heraklion.

Chloe and her father were familiar with the journey to Brindisi, having done it many times when visiting Panagiotis and Calliope. On the day of their departure, Charlotte drove them to Heathrow to catch an early-morning flight. Hugs and warm greetings awaited them as they were met at Brindisi airport by Panagiotis and his estate manager who drove them all to the port, near which they found a trattoria. The ferry did not leave until evening, allowing them the luxury of a leisurely late lunch, during which they made plans for the coming days.

Michalis and Chloe were famished after their early start. Panagiotis spent time perusing the wine list and chose a bottle of the fruity, light Malvasia from the Salento region. They tucked in to the rosemary-laced focaccia and ricotta polpette, followed by creamy cheese-and-garlic orecchiette and finished off with sweet pastry pasticciotti filled with custard. Panagiotis seemed circumspect about returning to his homeland. Any discomfort Michalis felt, he covered up with a business-like attitude towards the trip. Chloe, however, could not wait to visit the country which loomed so large in her heritage but which she knew so little about.

They agreed that on arrival they would spend the first day relaxing, recovering from their journey. When they had met with the lawyer and done all the necessary paperwork they would visit the land to assess its condition before finding an estate agent to handle the sale.

It was late afternoon by the time they paid the bill and were dropped off at the ferry terminal. Aboard the ship, Michalis took Panagiotis to find their cabin, whilst Chloe stood on deck watching the foot passengers climbing the gangways and huge lorries and cars crawling the creaking ramps into the bowels of the ship.

By the time the ferry had been loaded, the ramps winched up, gangways stowed and mooring lines cast off, the sun had set. The moon was full, illuminating the way as the ship left harbour. It sailed between the long protective arm of the Diga di Punta Riso and the small islands of Traversa and Pedagre, the lighthouse flashing green on the end of the long breakwater marking the start of the open sea.

Chloe stood at the rail, the warm evening air ruffling her long hair. She loved the sense of sailing into the unknown.

'I brought you a coffee.' Chloe turned to see her father holding out a cup. 'Black, no sugar.'

'Thanks, Dad.' She took the drink.

'Your grandfather has gone to bed. He's tired, and I don't think he particularly wants to be reminded of the last time we sailed these waters. If I'm honest, it doesn't bring back the happiest of memories for me either.' Michalis briefly related the story of how they had been pursued as they had made their escape to Italy all those years ago.

'What's there to worry about now? The Junta days are long gone,' Chloe reassured him.

'I know, it's ridiculous, but I still feel guilty that I was the cause of the fire,' said Michalis. 'If that hadn't happened, we wouldn't have lost everything.'

'Yes, and as I told you before, if it hadn't happened you wouldn't have Mum… or me.' Chloe took her father's hand.

'Of course, you're right, but at the time it was quite traumatic. I'm not going to let it spoil our time together on Crete, but I think for your grandfather it will be quite emotional, bringing back memories of his mum and dad. It was hard for your great-grandfather to leave the country he had fought so bravely to help liberate during the war.'

Chloe pushed a loose strand of hair behind her ear. She had been too young when her great-grandfather died to remember him, but knew from what her father had told her that he had led an extraordinary life. 'I understand how difficult it must be for both you and Grandad, but it's only for a week and then you can put all thoughts of Greece behind you.'

'I'm not sure we could ever do that,' replied Michalis. 'But I promise not to let it ruin our trip.'

Chloe put her arms around her father and hugged him tight. 'It'll be fine, Dad, just you see. Tell me some more about Grandad and the vineyard.'

Michalis sat down and Chloe joined him on a bench seat. He began hesitatingly, but as he got into the story he started to enjoy telling his daughter stories he himself had heard from his father, how Panagiotis and Christos had taken any jobs they could get, labouring or working in the fields for other farmers, to make money to survive whilst they were developing the vineyard in Epano Elounda. Any spare time they had they would clear their land of weeds and prune and train their vines as they established themselves on the hillside.

Back in those days, friends from the village came to help with the harvest, and nothing was wasted. The vine leaves were set aside to make dolmades, the cuttings stacked to provide fuel for the winter and later, after the grapes had been pressed, the residue would be distilled to make a spirit called raki.

'My grandparents Christos and Maria took care of me when Mum and Dad were busy working the land or making the wine. As soon as I could walk, I would play amongst the vines. Even from those early years I was intent on learning all I could and resolved to follow them into the family business.' Michalis surprised himself by bringing back happy memories from his boyhood in Epano Elounda.

He yawned and stretched. 'I'm exhausted. If you don't mind I think I'll head down to bed too.' Michalis stood and kissed his daughter on the head. '*Kalinichta,* I'll see you in the morning.'

Chloe felt relieved to see her father's smile as he turned and walked away.

She sipped her coffee as the lights of Brindisi faded to a faint glow before they disappeared. The sky above was dotted with more stars than Chloe thought she had ever seen. Looking down, the oil-flat sea reflected lights from the cabins on the lower decks. She knew she really should go below and catch some sleep but was relishing the moment, reluctant to let it go.

*

Chloe awoke early, eager to see the ship make landfall. Resuming her position at the rail on deck she watched the lights on Corfu as the ship coasted the narrow channel between the island and Albania. As dawn broke, the sun reflected off the sea and warmed her face. She was joined by her father and grandfather bearing coffee, and the three of them stood watching as the ship made its approach to the town of Kerkyra. How alike each other the two men were, Chloe thought, her father tall, muscular and tanned from a lifetime working in the open air. Her grandfather, now slightly stooped and greying, still had a glint in his eye which revealed his lust for life.

Despite the hour, the quayside was bustling. They had time to spare before their flight, so they took a taxi into the Old Town to find breakfast. In the early-morning sun the flaking, honey-coloured, medieval buildings of the Campiello entranced Chloe and she recognised the influence of the Italians who had held sway here for so many years – but it was different. Something in the light changed everything. She immediately knew she had left the mannered ways and manicured vistas of Italy behind and was in a country that was already special to her. It was as though she had opened her eyes and the world had been reborn.

Beneath the imposing dome of the church of St Spyridon, they made their way through the maze of alleyways, passages and small squares before emerging on a colonnaded terrace. Filled with cafés it looked out over an expanse of green, bordered by flowerbeds in glorious bloom. If the architecture of the Campiello was Venetian in style, this reminded Chloe of Paris. She pulled out her phone and searched, discovering that this was the Liston, a pastiche of the Rue de Rivoli, built by the French in the early nineteenth century. Chloe was even more curious to learn that on the green in front of them, cricket was played; a legacy of the time when Britain governed Corfu.

As they sat eating breakfast, Panagiotis was reflective, only speaking to answer his granddaughter's questions about the island. Michalis was eager to get to the airport and kept looking at his watch but Chloe felt as though the world was slowing down. As her body warmed with the rising sun, she experienced a sense of belonging.

It took a while for the waiter to bring the bill. As they walked to a taxi rank, Michalis was concerned they would be late for their plane. But it turned out the airport was close to town and they arrived with time to spare. A short stopover in Athens and they were taking off again on the final leg of the journey. Chloe commandeered the window seat and sat looking down on the water below studded with islands, while sailing boats, fishing craft, ships and ferries drew patterns in white across the surface.

It seemed no sooner had they taken off than they began descending towards Heraklion. Chloe could make out small figures aboard the vessels below and, as they got closer to the island, people on the golden sands, and olive trees covering the hillsides. Sweeping over a beach and just metres above a clifftop, the plane dropped onto the runway. Chloe was pinned back into her seat by the braking of the aircraft as it slowed rapidly before turning towards the terminal.

Stepping out of the plane, she felt the heat hit her and inhaled the salt air laced with oregano, thyme and other herbs from the mountains. Something came over her, as though the land was in her blood. This was the place she had heard about in the stories her father and grandfather had told.

On the bus that took them to the terminal the men were silent, engrossed in their own emotions. But their luggage was soon on the carousel and as they stepped out of the airport, they seemed to relax.

In no time they had picked up the rental car and Michalis carefully negotiated the traffic, finding his way onto the national highway leading east. The road wove round and cut through the mountains which skirted the sea. Panagiotis did not recognise the coastal plain which had once been fruit orchards but was now covered with hotels, apartments and the holiday villas of resorts which appeared to merge into one another. Inland, though, olive groves still clung to the hillsides, dotted with sugar-cube villages.

Leaving the resorts behind, the road rose and followed the course of a wooded ravine where walls and wire cages had been constructed along the roadside as protection from boulders that might fall from the mountains above. Near the top of the gorge, nestling in the forested slopes, Chloe could make out a bell tower poking through the trees. She noticed her grandfather make the sign of the cross as they passed.

'What is that?' Chloe broke the silence.

'It's the monastery of Agios Georgios, Selinari,' answered Panagiotis from the front seat. 'When we used to go to Heraklion, we always knew that when we got here on our way back, we were nearing home. Saint George is the saint of travellers and it is thought good luck to stop or at least cross yourself as you pass.'

At the top of the gorge, Chloe felt they had moved into a different world, wilder, more rugged and remote. Skeletons of windmills, long since abandoned, stood by the roadside. Orchards of almond trees and groves of silver-leaved olives cascaded down the mountainsides. Approaching the top of a hill, Chloe noticed the lookout tower and austere barbed wire-capped walls of what her father confirmed was a prison. For Michalis and his father it brought unwanted thoughts of what could have been their fate had they not escaped from the Junta.

Michalis drove the last few kilometres to Agios Nikolaos in silence. The city had changed a lot. He had to concentrate hard to find his way through the busy streets to the port where they would park the car. The hotel was on the harbour, reached up steps lined with potted plants bursting with colour. Their rooms had Juliet balconies looking out on the waterfront and the Bay of Mirabello stretching beyond. All three were tired after the journey and agreed to go to their rooms for a siesta. Chloe was itching to get out and explore the city, but even she had to admit to being worn out.

She collapsed on her bed, the shutters and windows still open, the room flooded in sunlight and a breeze blowing the net curtains. Exhausted, she fell into a deep sleep.

It was dark when she awoke. It took her a moment to realise where she was. She crossed the room and looked out of the window. She could see the lights of a giant cruise ship towering above the quayside. Below, the street was alive with people and the warm evening air was filled with the noise of car horns and motorbikes.

She heard a knock on the door.

'I haven't disturbed you, have I?' asked her father.

'No, I've just woken up,' replied Chloe.

'I was wondering if you would like to go out and find something to eat? I asked Grandad, but he said he was still tired. It's been a long day for him. He'll feel better for a good sleep.'

'Just give me ten minutes to freshen up and I'll meet you in reception.' Chloe was eager to see a bit more of the town.

There were far more tavernas than Michalis could remember from the days of his youth. Agios Nikolaos had fully embraced tourism and everything it had to offer. But its essence hadn't changed much. It was vibrant but remained welcoming and relaxed. One thing totally unchanged was the beautiful lake at the heart of the town, connected to the harbour by a narrow canal. Chloe was enchanted. The lights from the tavernas and cafés illuminated the small caiques moored around the lagoon. Behind the lake was a cliff beneath which was a tiny white chapel cut into the hillside.

Michalis picked a taverna which had a table right by the water. Chloe listened as her father spoke Greek, chatting to the waiters. She noticed how he had slipped back into his native tongue as though he had never been away. At home in England he had made a point of speaking the language to her so she learned it, and when they were in Italy he would use it when speaking to his parents. Chloe was fairly fluent, but was pleased the menu was also written in English as she struggled reading the language.

The waiter brought water and Michalis ordered a jug of cold, dry, light red wine to accompany the *stifado* they both had chosen. Chloe was ravenous and devoured the beef which was slow-cooked in wine, tomatoes, onions and herbs, the dark chunks of meat melting in her mouth. She was too full to take up her father's offer of a dessert, but the waiter brought a plate of watermelon, apple and banana and a small carafe of an icy, clear spirit which her father told her was raki.

'It's made from what's left over after the grapes are processed to make wine, as I mentioned yesterday. They don't do what we do in England, and make organic fertiliser to go back on the land,' he laughed. 'All the residue from the presses is distilled to make this.'

Michalis poured out the raki and raised a glass to his daughter. '*Yammas!*' He downed the spirit in one.

'*Yammas.*' Chloe raised her glass and took a sip. She felt the liquid burn in her throat as it went down. 'It's probably an acquired taste, but something I think I could get used to,' she said, laughing, throwing back her head and emptying the glass.

Michalis filled both glasses again. Chloe relaxed into her comfy chair and took in the scene in front of her. All around the lake people were sitting, eating and drinking. A small caique was heading for the canal, the fisherman ducking to get under the low bridge. An elderly lady wove her way from taverna to taverna selling lace tablecloths and children cycled along the waterfront. A priest greeted the waiter and accepted his invitation to stop for a drink, sitting and lighting a cigarette.

'I like it here.' Chloe yawned.

'We've got all day tomorrow to explore before we meet the lawyer the next day,' said Michalis. 'Shall we head back to the hotel?'

Chloe slept soundly, and rose to the noises of the town waking up: traffic on the streets below and traders readying their businesses for the day ahead. She opened the shutters and the sun came streaming into the room, reflecting off whitewashed walls. It had rained overnight and the day smelled fresh and new. She quickly showered and left the room, almost running down the stone steps. She headed for a large café she had noticed the previous evening and ordered three coffees and pastries to take away. Returning to the hotel, she found both her father and grandfather were up and grateful for the breakfast. Chloe was keen to get out and explore.

'I'll wait here whilst you two have a look around,' said Panagiotis. The town's a bit hilly for me these days and I'm quite happy to sit here reading. Pick me up when it's time for lunch.'

Chloe could see what her grandfather had meant as they walked around the lake to the small chapel and began to ascend the path which traversed the cliff. Out of breath, she stopped and waited for her father to catch up, and the view back down to the lake and out across the bay brought a smile to her face.

They strolled to the old square where the lawyer they were meeting the following day had her office, before going downhill to a beach surrounded by cafés where they stopped for a cold drink. Following the coast road, a headland was adorned by a striking statue. The sinuous sculpture of copper and glass came to a point which punctured the clear blue sky.

'I don't remember this being here when I was a boy,' said Michalis, reading the plaque. Called Almathea's Horn, it represented the cornucopia provided for Crete by both land and sea.

Walking on, they arrived back at the port and in the car park stood another immense sculpture, a giant bronze called the Abduction of Europa, according to the plaque.

'This is new as well,' said Michalis.

'Well, you haven't been here for forty years, Dad, so it's hardly surprising some things have changed.'

Michalis explained the legend of Europa, proudly telling his daughter how the first Queen of Crete and the Minoans also had given her name to the continent of Europe. As he spoke, Chloe could see a light in her father's eyes as he stared out across the bay, taking in the small island of Agioi Pandes then turning to gaze at the mountains stretching all the way to the far east of the island.

'We should go and find your grandfather. He'll be wanting some lunch.' Michalis started along the waterfront to the hotel. 'There was a restaurant near the town beach that looked good. If we ask the receptionist to get us a taxi, I'm sure Grandad would enjoy it.'

The restaurant was right on the seafront, looking across a small bay to a beach and the headland where the sculpture of Almathea's Horn stood against a backdrop of a blue that was almost impossible for Chloe to comprehend. All three of them were hungry and asked for a platter of fish to share: crispy squid, rich octopus, striped mackerel, smoky sea bass from the grill and a large carafe of ice-cold, dry white wine.

Chloe could not remember ever having been more relaxed. When Panagiotis and Michalis went back to the hotel for a siesta, she wandered alone around the town, so captivated that the hours slipped by. As dusk fell, she crossed the bridge over the cutting which connected the lake to the harbour. A tiny fishing boat motored its way seawards to join the few other caiques fishing, their lights twinkling in the bay.

The air was cooling as she set out along the tree-lined esplanade leading out of town. She thought of how her father and grandfather had been forced to flee this paradise in fear of their lives and how those memories must be playing on their minds. She knew they were anxious about the next day's proceedings but hoped that with the business of the vineyard out of the way they would be able to enjoy their last few days on

Crete. She was looking forward to discovering more of the island she was falling in love with.

At a café she sat and ordered a coffee. Around her, tables were full of tourists enjoying an evening drink. Out to sea, a lighthouse on a tiny island flashed its light and a thousand stars glittered in the night sky above.

Chapter 8

CHLOE AWOKE TO a clear, crisp sky with a hint of autumn in the air but all the promise of a hot day. Agios Nikolaos sparkled like a gem in the early-morning light. She reluctantly dragged herself from the balcony to shower and get ready for the meeting which had been set for ten that morning. She found herself singing as she showered, then debated with herself what to wear, deciding on a white dress and trainers. Her hair would dry in the sun she thought, pulling a brush through it before she skipped down the steps to join her father and grandfather in the hotel reception.

They ascended the pedestrianised street from the harbour as shopkeepers put out displays of jewellery, clothes, pottery, herbs and anything else which might catch the eye of tourists.

Panagiotis strolled alone with his thoughts, taking his time. Chloe bubbled over with enthusiasm.

She had always been a cheerful child, thought Michalis, but here in Crete something was different. The island appeared to fit her, bringing her alive in a way he hadn't seen before. He listened contentedly to his daughter's commentary as they went, answering any questions as best he could.

At the top of the hill the road flattened and opened out onto a small square. Traffic jostled on a roundabout encircling a marble memorial guarded by four large palm trees and a box cut hedge. In one corner rose a magnificent church. A sign above a nearby shop confirmed they had arrived at the lawyer's office.

Ringing the bell, they were buzzed through the door. They climbed the stairs to the first floor to be greeted by the solicitor, who introduced herself as Georgia. Her smile eased the formality as she ushered them into her office and they settled into chairs, her assistant offering to get them coffee.

With introductions completed, Georgia explained that the ownership of the vineyard was not disputed by her client, but if Panagiotis thought it necessary he should get his own legal representation. She confirmed that she was acting on behalf of Tassos' daughter, Sofia, who was eager to get the matter sorted.

The mention of the name gave Michalis a start. He wondered what Sofia's life was like now.

On first impressions Panagiotis liked the lawyer and, as there was no dispute over the land, he felt it would be better to keep the business simple and deal with just the one solicitor. 'If the boundaries are agreed between us and the other party, I think we should get the matter dealt with as quickly as possible,' he told her. 'I intend to instruct an agent to put the land up for sale as soon as the deeds are put into my name anyway.'

The paperwork was laborious, with Panagiotis having to show his passport and numerous forms of identity alongside his parents' death certificates. Georgia made light of the process and, after what seemed like an eternity, the last form was signed. She told Panagiotis that he needed to open a bank account if he intended to sell the property and led them across the road to a bank. Panagiotis was pleased he had Georgia with him as with every form the clerk requested he fill in, a heated discussion ensued about the detail. It was like a war of attrition which the experienced Georgia was resolved to win, and she did as the clock ticked down to lunchtime and the clerk bundled up the paperwork, photocopied it and declared the account open.

Georgia assured them that the ordeal was nearly over as she guided them to another office to see the notary. The kindly woman offered them water and sweets and after numerous further papers were signed and a cash payment for her services made, the process was complete. Panagiotis now officially owned what had been his father's vineyard. Returning to her office, Georgia offered to conveyance the property when Panagiotis was ready to sell and told him that she could recommend an agent. He scribbled down the number and, shaking hands, thanked Georgia for her help and agreed to contact her when the plot was put on the market.

Outside, Panagiotis passed the number of the estate agent to Michalis, asking him to ring right away and see if they could make an appointment.

'Is this afternoon alright?' Michalis asked his father. 'He suggests we meet at three in Elounda and we can drive up to the village together to show him where it is.'

'That's fine, there's no point in putting it off. And it gives us time for lunch first.'

The agent recommended a taverna near the harbour in Elounda and arranged to meet them there. On the walk back down the hill towards where they had parked the hire car, Michalis could see his father was pensive. He too did not know how he was going to react seeing his childhood home again. Chloe could sense the apprehension in the two men she adored most in the world. As they walked, she wrapped an arm around each of them.

Michalis drove them away from the centre along the esplanade where Chloe had sat the previous evening. He knew the way by instinct and although the view was familiar it was also foreign to him. The clear blue waters and the two islands offshore which they had sailed past as they made their escape all those years ago were unchanged, but the outskirts of the town had sprouted hotels and tavernas on what he remembered as countryside. The autumn sun was still warm and tourists strolled the waterfront, the cafés and bars doing steady trade.

Leaving the town, the road climbed steeply up a mountainside. Beneath them the cliffs fell away to the cobalt sea. Turning her head, Chloe could see the coast curling around the Bay of Mirabello and then unfolding in the haze for miles towards the east. She could not help grinning at the view; but if that enraptured Chloe, what awaited her as they reached the summit took her breath away.

Spread out in front of them lay the Bay of Korfos, the mountainside dotted with villas and far below the small town of Elounda glistening beside the enamel sea. In the distance at the entrance to the bay floated a small island, which her father said was Spinalonga. Small boats drew filigree patterns of silver across the azure surface of the water as they criss-crossed their way to and from the island. Panagiotis sat silent, and Chloe was sure she could see a tear in her grandfather's eye.

The road dropped steeply towards sea level and narrowed through a street of shops, bars and apartments. Michalis had to weave the car around pedestrians and parked vehicles before emerging at a square beside a small harbour, where they stopped. The quay was lined with caiques painted in bright colours, and the tables and chairs of tavernas and cafés spilt out onto the square.

Chloe was quickly out of the back seat and could not stop beaming as she stood on the waterfront. A fisherman was mending his nets, a cat asleep in the shade of the bench on which he sat. A church tower with a terracotta tiled roof and belfry stood surrounded by palm trees. Chloe turned back to the car and saw her father and grandfather getting out and looking around, taking in how the view had changed since they had left a lifetime ago. She thought she could detect the hint of a smile on both their faces.

'That's the place,' Michalis said, pointing purposefully towards the taverna the estate agent had recommended. 'Come over when you're ready.'

Confronted by the menu and confounded by the choice, they decided to order a selection of mixed mezzes. The dishes just kept coming: pitta bread, hummus, tzatziki, aubergine salad, halloumi cheese, village sausage, stuffed vine leaves, falafel, meatballs in tomato sauce, bite-sized horta pies, giant beans and a Greek salad served with a large carafe of white wine.

They ate mostly in silence, each with their own thoughts. For Panagiotis, being in Elounda brought back memories of his childhood and his parents; Michalis was thinking about how things might have been had life taken a different turn; and Chloe was more contented than ever before. It felt like she had found her spiritual home.

Panagiotis looked at the joy on his granddaughter's face and could no longer keep quiet. 'Your father and I were talking yesterday when you were out exploring.'

Chloe looked up from her plate and took a sip of her wine.

'We want you to have the proceeds from the sale of the land. I don't expect it will be worth a lot, but it might help you to put down a deposit on your own home back in England.'

'Oh no, I couldn't accept that, Grandad,' said Chloe, shocked.

'We both want you to have it. Take it as a thank you for all the help you have given me over the years bringing in the harvest. I am old and comfortably off, and will not live forever.' Panagiotis looked at his son. 'Your parents already have a successful business and have no need for the money so have agreed that whatever I get for the land is yours, Chloe.'

She could see from the determination on her grandfather's face that his mind was made up and that he would brook no arguments. Chloe rounded the table and hugged him tight.

*

Squeezing into the back of the hire car, the suited estate agent joined them as Michalis drove out of the square and onto the narrow road which climbed the mountain. On either side, olive trees tumbled down the hillside, glittering as they rustled in the afternoon breeze. Through the open windows Chloe could hear the stop-go chorus of cicadas and the tinkle of bells from goats grazing high above. She noticed her grandfather turn his head and look as they passed signs announcing the village of Epano Elounda, but her father kept his eyes ahead on the road as they climbed higher. Above the village he swung the car onto a track just wide enough to be accessible and they bumped along until he brought them to a halt on a flat clearing.

Chloe noticed the emotion on her grandfather and father's faces as they got out of the car. Through the overgrown vines she could see the remains of what once she supposed had been their home. She pushed aside the wild plants and approached the forlorn remains of the house. Closing her eyes she tried to imagine how it would have been. The stone was warm to her touch. She opened her eyes and turned, letting out a gasp. From where she stood she could see all the way down the mountainside. In the distance she could make out a causeway which appeared to be floating on the water, and a bridge crossing a canal which joined the bay to Mirabello beyond. What a wonderful place this must have been for her family to live. How agonising it must have been to be forced to leave.

Panagiotis approached the shell of what had been his home, back when his own parents were alive; the house he'd grown up in, the vineyard he'd worked with his father; the house he and Calliope had lived in when they were first married, where Michalis was born and raised. It looked smaller than he remembered. He pulled aside the tendrils of vines, revealing the walls. Nothing remained of the roof, which had collapsed in the fire all those years ago, or the windows and doors, which had burned to a cinder. Looking up the mountainside, what Panagiotis remembered as ordered lines of vines was now a jungle of plants fighting to strangle each other.

In silence they followed the estate agent as he tried to determine the extent of the property. They walked along the drystone wall skirting the narrow road, following it uphill for a hundred metres. Michalis pulled away at the vines where he recalled the boundary between their vineyard and that of their neighbour's had once been. Within minutes, moving aside stems and leaves, he found it, the clear footprint of the wall which had marked the extent of their land. Although Tassos had demolished it, he had been too lazy to dig out the stones of its foundations.

The estate agent went off alone, pacing out the perimeter and scribbling notes in his pad. Michalis put an arm over his father's shoulder as they returned down the hillside to the remains of the house. At the boundary, Chloe could not take her eyes off the view. Despite the afternoon heat, a soft, cooling breeze blew up the mountainside, caressing the ripening olives, and down in the bay she could still see boats crossing to and from Spinalonga. She looked at the tangle of plants fighting for space to flourish, noticing how different they were from the clipped ranks of pampered vines on her grandparents' and parents' vineyards.

Walking back down, she joined Panagiotis and her father in the courtyard of what had once been their home and winery. Chloe could imagine what the buildings had been like before the arson attack, and began to understand their melancholy. She walked around the ruins. A tree had taken root inside the house, its branches stretching above where the roof had once been. The render was discoloured, cracked and flaked away under her touch, and the ground was littered with old bottles and plastic carrier bags. But behind the crumbling render the stone walls had stood firm, enough for her to picture in her mind's eye what the house must have looked like.

'What do you think?' Chloe heard her grandfather ask the agent who had joined them in the skeleton of the old buildings.

'As I see it you have two options,' he started. 'The land as it stands has a value, of course, but to make it attractive to any potential buyers in the current market the price will need to be low, as it requires a lot of work to make it usable to farm or be developed. If you undertook to have that work done and restored the buildings it might be worth a considerable amount more, but that would take a lot of time and money.'

'I'm sorry, Chloe.' Panagiotis seemed upset. 'We appear to have gifted you a pig in a poke.'

'Would you mind if I kept it?' The words left her mouth before she had time to think but as soon as she said them, she realised it was something she dearly wanted. Since being on the island, she had experienced a sense of belonging she could never have imagined. She had always been happy, but here on Crete something felt right, as though it was meant to be.

For a moment both her father and Panagiotis remained silent. The thought had come to her so quickly that she had not considered how they might react. There was a slight glimmer in her grandfather's eyes but her father looked concerned. Neither dismissed her idea out of hand though.

'I think we need some time to discuss our options,' Panagiotis said to the agent, who hid his disappointment well. 'If you let me have your figures I will get back in touch before we leave in a couple of days.'

They drove back down the mountain in silence, until they reached the place where the agent had left his car in Elounda.

'Thank you for your time. I'll give you a call soon.' Panagiotis raised a hand as the man got into his car. Then he turned to the others. 'I think we need a chat,' he suggested. 'And maybe a closer look at the land. Let's go back and check it out, then maybe take a look around the village before we consider things more carefully.'

Chloe could feel her excitement rising as they drove back up the winding road. In turn, her grandfather could sense in himself a warmth at the unexpected turn of events. Michalis was confused, wondering what his wife would say if he returned from the trip with their daughter having decided to emigrate to Greece.

Back at the old vineyard, with the possibilities Chloe's idea had opened up, Panagiotis could not help feel the pull of the land, despite the way his old neighbour had squeezed so many vines onto the plot that they were weak and fighting each other to survive.

Michalis stood for some time before wandering off and examining the vines. He was in two minds. He had always given his daughter the freedom to pursue her dreams, but this was a long way from her family in England and the task was immense. Up the hillside he could make out the house where Tassos had lived until recently, and he shuddered at that thought. Yet he had noticed a change in his daughter since arriving in Greece and now it was impossible to ignore the fact that the more she saw of the land, the more enthusiastic she became.

For the moment he put aside his reservations and tried to take a dispassionate view of the business possibilities the land might offer. He reminded himself of the extent of the plot, and in his head calculated how many healthy vines it would sustain and the grapes they might yield. Bending down he examined the ground, letting the dry earth run through his fingers.

Chloe looked around, her head churning with ideas for the vineyard. She was excited by the prospect of taking on the project but at the same time daunted. What had she got to lose though? Now the harvests were in at her father and grandfather's vineyards she was at a loose end. She needed a new challenge. She found it hard to tear herself away, but when her grandfather suggested they look around Epano Elounda she was keen to see the village.

As they pulled up and parked outside the village church, Panagiotis felt a shiver pass through him. He had never thought he would return here again. Getting out, almost instinctively he took the narrow path leading to the lanes which wove their way through the village, and Michalis and Chloe followed.

A number of the houses looked abandoned, their disintegrating doors vainly padlocked; some were ramshackle, but glancing through the open shutters revealed signs of life. Others had been restored, their walls gleaming white and window frames and doors freshly painted. A wild fig tree had forced its way through a crack in the path and a bright pink bougainvillea covered the wall of a well-tended small cottage. Panagiotis struggled to remember who had lived where, yet the village streets resembled the images from the past which he held in his mind. He knew what he was looking and maybe even hoping for.

Rounding the corner of the narrow street which ran through the centre of the village he saw it. The door to the taverna stood open.

Behind the counter, looking at his phone, was a sturdy man with a head of black hair. Digging into the depths of his memory, Michalis remembered him as Alexander, a boy he had gone to the local school with as a child. They had grown up playing in the alleys and olive groves together.

The man looked up. His face broke into a smile of recognition.

'Michali, is it really you? When I heard about Tassos I wondered what would happen to the land, but after all this time, I never thought we would see you again. And Panagioti, how good to see you too.'

'Your father?' Panagiotis asked quietly.

'Sadly passed, he's been dead nearly twenty years.'

'I'm sorry for your loss.'

'It's been a long time now. Let's not dwell on that. Sit and have a drink. It's wonderful to see you. And this is?'

'I'm sorry. This is Chloe, my daughter.' said Michalis. The beaming Alexander came out from behind the counter and shook her hand.

The last time Panagiotis and Michalis had been in the taverna was after their attempt to extinguish the fire that had engulfed the vineyard, the night they had fled the village. Too much had happened in the intervening years to recall. The gap was too wide to bridge with words so for the time being they sat together toasting their families, the marriages and children that had been born and those they had lost. As evening drew in, the taverna began to fill up and Alexander had to leave the table to cook and serve the customers.

'Are you serious about the vineyard?' Now the three of them were alone together, Panagiotis broached the subject with Chloe.

'I think I am, Grandad. I've trained to make wine and have worked with you and Dad in your vineyards for as long as I can remember. But more than that, coming here I've felt a connection which I can't explain. I feel a belonging, that this is the place I was meant to be.' Chloe turned towards her father who was looking down at his hands which were clutched together in his lap. 'Dad, it's not the other end of the earth. I can easily fly back to England, and you and Mum could come here.'

'If it's what you want, you know neither your mother nor I would stand in your way. But please don't decide until you have spoken to her. I'll call her later and have a chat. If you are still sure, you can phone her and tell her your plans. You have a lot of thinking to do.'

'Why not sleep on it and let us know what you decide in the morning?' said Panagiotis. 'It's been a long day, and I don't know about you but I'm tired. Do you mind if we go back to the hotel?'

They stood to leave and Alexander came from behind the counter to say goodbye. They reassured him that it would not be another forty years before they saw him again. Alone with their own thoughts, they drove in the darkness down the hillside to the bright lights of Elounda. Leaving the small town behind, Chloe turned and looked back at the lights on the causeway stretching out to the bridge and the looming darkness of the hills which encircled the bay before the car topped the mountain and descended towards Agios Nikolaos.

It had been a spur-of-the-moment decision by Chloe to suggest she keep the vineyard, but alone in her room at the hotel, the reality of the situation began to dawn on her. She had some savings which might stretch to supporting her whilst she cleared the land, but not enough to rebuild the house and winery, let alone buying de-stalkers, presses, vats, barrels and bottles. This would have to be a very long-term project. Maybe after she had cleared the land she could get a job whilst she saved to do the building work and establish new vines. She lay in bed, thoughts spinning around her head. She did not know how she would make her dream come true but was steadfast that she would try.

Chapter 9

SHE MUST HAVE finally succumbed to sleep, and awoke to the ring of her mobile phone. Reaching out to the bedside table she blinked at the screen. It was eight o'clock. What was her dad doing calling her at this time?

'Good morning. Your grandfather and I thought you might like breakfast. We've got you a croissant and a pastry and are sitting on the esplanade if you'd like to join us. It's a beautiful day.'

Within minutes Chloe had showered, dressed and run down the steps to the waterfront. The road was quiet as she crossed the bridge separating the lake from the harbour to find her father and grandfather. Soon she saw them, deep in conversation, sitting on a bench beneath a tamarisk tree.

'Good morning, couldn't you sleep?' Chloe greeted them, sitting down.

'We thought it was such a beautiful day that we would have breakfast on the front.' Michalis handed her a bag and a takeaway cup of coffee. 'How did you sleep?'

'I got off eventually, but it took me some time. I was thinking things over.'

'And how do you feel now about taking on the vineyard?' asked Panagiotis.

'I know you think I'm mad, but I think I can make a go of it. I would regret it if I didn't try.'

The two men listened as Chloe told them of her plans. Even as she was saying it, what had seemed like a good idea the night before now appeared a formidable prospect when said out loud. Seeing a drop in her spirits, her father could keep her waiting no longer.

'Last night your grandfather and I had a chat with Mum.' Michalis took out his phone and dialled a number before putting it on speaker and laying it on the bench.

'What sort of time in the morning do you call this?' Chloe heard her mother laughing at the other end of the phone.

'Oops, sorry love, I forgot the time difference,' Michalis apologised.

'Don't worry, I couldn't really sleep and was waiting for you to call. Are Chloe and Panagiotis there?' asked Charlotte.

'Yes, we're here. How are you, Mum?' Chloe replied.

'I'm excited. Last night your dad and grandad told me about your crazy plans, and we've come up with an idea which might make them slightly more feasible. We'd all like to come into partnership with you, if you'll have us? The vineyard would still be yours but we could invest to help you get things up and running.'

For a moment, Chloe was speechless.

'Are you there?' she heard her mother ask.

'Yes. Yes! Of course. Thank you. Thank you!'

'Then we've got a deal. You talk it through with Dad and Grandad and I'll get back to bed. We'll speak soon. Love you all.' The phone went dead.

Chloe flung her arms around her father and hugged him before standing and doing the same to Panagiotis. Sitting back down on the bench beside the sea in the shade of the tree, she listened as her father explained the ideas they had outlined in their discussion the previous evening.

Michalis told her that they proposed to merge their businesses with her fledgling vineyard. Her grandfather and parents would keep control of their own operations but would provide investment and marketing opportunities to Chloe's new venture. Panagiotis told her how he was not getting any younger and that his business would eventually fall to his son, and along with her mother and father's business would eventually be left to her anyway. It made sense to give her the financial help she needed now to make the vineyard a success.

Panagiotis excused himself and walked along the seafront. Leaning against the rail he stared out to sea before reaching in his pocket for his mobile phone. He phoned Calliope to let her know the news. Her reaction was as he had expected: his wife was as excited as he was that the land would remain in the family.

Michalis still had his doubts about the viability of the vineyard in today's tough market, but kept his counsel. Charlotte had said it was a great opportunity for their daughter to make her way in the world and that although she would miss her, Crete was not that far away, and they had to cut the apron strings sometime. Michalis was happy to go along with the idea if it made his daughter happy, and being in partnership he could at least keep an eye on how things were going for her.

They talked about how they could ship out vats and barrels from England that stood redundant after Michalis had switched his production to sparkling wine and also how they could merge brands and try to bring wine produced in the Cretan village to Britain and beyond. But they were getting ahead of themselves, that would be years in the future. First they needed to cost out the work required to clear and replant the land and make the burned-down house habitable.

Chloe was fired up with ideas, and found herself swinging between enthusiasm and anxiety at the task ahead. 'Dad, do you mind if I take the car and go up to the vineyard? I'd like to make some notes and start planning.'

'I'll come with you.' Michalis stood, but his father reached out for his arm.

'Let her go by herself,' Panagiotis told his son quietly.

Reaching in his pocket, Michalis handed his daughter the keys. 'We'll see you later.'

*

Chloe's mind had been racing with possibilities, but as she got out of the car beside the burned-out remains of the farmhouse and winery, the scale of what she had taken on overwhelmed her. She turned away from the blighted buildings and looked down the mountainside to the bay, took a deep breath and delved in her bag for a notebook. It was best to begin with practicalities before any negative thoughts took hold.

She wrote all the things that needed doing. The list seemed endless. But the very act of scribbling things down made Chloe feel she was making progress. She divided the list into work that was required on the land and the building work.

It made sense to start on the land. Firstly, she needed to rebuild the wall between the vineyard and her neighbour's property. Chloe knew that at the very least the vines needed thinning and possibly replacing totally. It would take at least three years until any new plants would yield a significant harvest and she could even begin using them to make wine.

She would test the soil and research the best grape varieties for the terroir; later she would seek her grandfather's advice on that. Being on a hillside, she knew the land would drain well but the vines had been squeezed onto the plot and were choking each other, fighting for light and nutrition from the soil rather than being spaced apart, aligned north to south. Her instincts told her to hedge her bets by growing grapes to produce white, red and rosé.

As she wanted to plant the new vines in the spring, she would have her work cut out to prepare the land in six months, but she was a hard worker and with the investment from her parents and grandparents, maybe she could hire some labour to help.

Once the vines were in the ground she could turn her attention to the building. She was no expert, but it appeared to her that the walls of the house and winery were sound. Once the roofs had been replaced and new windows and doors put in to make the buildings weatherproof, she would be able to do much of the decorating herself.

Making a list helped organise her thoughts. If she started at the top and worked through it gradually, perhaps things would be less daunting. Her father and grandfather were leaving in a couple of days, and if she was staying on she would need to find somewhere to live. The hotel was too far away and too expensive long-term. With the end of the tourist season approaching, maybe there was somewhere she could rent in the village at a reasonable price?

She followed the path that wove its way through the adjoining olive groves, descending towards the terracotta roofs of the village. She was happy in her own company. Although she would miss her family and friends, she was used to travelling on her own and knew she would not be lonely. In the distance she heard the sound of bells, and looking up she could see a line of goats traversing the hillside, herded by a large black dog. Below her the sapphire bay glistened in the midday sun.

From the edge of the village, Chloe kept strolling downhill. She recognised the narrow main street, which she followed until she reached the taverna. Alexander immediately remembered her. He greeted her like an old friend before bringing water and taking her order of salad and dakos and a glass of wine. She decided to try her luck, and asked if he happened to know if there was somewhere she could rent in the village. Before she had finished her lunch he had made a phone call and arranged for her to see a small flat.

Only a minute's walk from the taverna she found the apartment, the elderly landlady waiting for her with the key. The outside looked newly painted, the walls white and the door, shutters and window frames in the traditional blue used in the village. Around the door climbed a bougainvillea, its pink petals carpeting the step which led to the front door. It was perfect. The main living space was simply furnished with a bed, table, chair and a small wardrobe, and was separated from the kitchen by a breakfast bar. The cooking facilities were basic, with a stove running off bottled gas, but there was a fridge and a small selection of pots and pans. A door from the kitchen led to a shower room which was tiny but bright and clean. The flat had everything Chloe needed and it was cheap. Rather than drive on the road she could walk up the mountain track to the vineyard which would take her less than twenty minutes and when she was tired after a day's work it would be a downhill stroll home.

When Chloe returned to Agios Nikolaos, she told her father she had rented somewhere to live and was staying on. Michalis was shocked at how fast things were developing, but Panagiotis reminded him of their own enthusiasm to establish the vineyard in Italy when they arrived there as refugees and also how hard he had worked to make a success of the business in England.

'You should be proud that she's keen to get started – it'll be quite a few years as you know before the business will make any money.'

Over dinner that evening, Chloe talked through her plans. In the time they had left on Crete, Panagiotis said he would buy a kit to test the soil. He was interested to see if things had changed since he had planted the land with his father. He also agreed to ask the estate agent if he could recommend a builder to take on the restoration of the house. Michalis was eager to take his daughter's rough notes and turn them into a costed business plan.

Chloe wanted to get some bits and pieces in town the next morning to make her flat a home, so they agreed to meet up for lunch before driving out to the vineyard. Michalis stayed up long into the night working on figures and in the morning went with his father to the solicitor to set in motion the transference of deeds, before driving to the agricultural merchants to buy a soil-testing kit.

Meanwhile, Chloe found a shop near the yacht marina where she bought sheets, a duvet for the winter and pillowcases. Resolved to stand on her own two feet, she then went to the bank to open an account. She was patient and after an hour or so had achieved what she had set out to do. By the time the three met up at a taverna by the lake it felt as though they had already made progress. Looking over the plan Michalis had drawn up and agreeing to go and test the soil in the afternoon, Chloe felt they were moving forward.

'I'm pleased you opened a bank account Chloe,' said Michalis, reaching in his pocket for an envelope, leaning across the table and handing it to his daughter. 'This is the first instalment of your grandfather's and our investment. To get you started it's a cheque for twenty thousand euros, which will pay your rent and the initial builders' invoices. When the land is ready for planting we can assess the next instalment.'

For a moment Chloe was speechless, her face lit up in delight. 'Thank you. I don't know what to say.'

'You don't need to say anything. We have faith that you will make a go of the business,' said Panagiotis. 'Let's go up to the vineyard to start work.'

*

'Top of your list was rebuilding the boundary wall. We also need to clear a tract of land so your vines aren't at risk from any infection from the neighbour's crop, such as it is,' Michalis told his daughter. Let's go up the hill and take a look while Grandad tests the soil. He's dying to to use the new kit.'

Father and daughter walked up the hillside on the narrow road which followed the edge of the property until they reached the remains of the old wall.

'The first thing we'll have to order is a whole load of new stone to rebuild the wall. That won't be cheap,' Chloe said.

'Hold on a minute.' Michalis stepped onto the neighbour's land and pulled aside the mass of vines and leaves to reveal rocks scattered on the ground. 'I thought as much. Tassos was too lazy to have moved them far away. It'll be hard work, but the stone is probably all here to rebuild it.' He bent down and lifted a rock and moved it to where the wall had stood.

Chloe joined him, feeling with her feet for the stones, lifting one up and placing it alongside her father's. 'It'll take some time,' she said, 'but I think I can manage enough to remark the boundary, then I can work clearing our land and maybe go online and learn how to build back the wall bit by bit.'

Returning down the mountainside, they found Panagiotis leaning on the car, scribbling in his notebook. 'The earth here is slightly acidic and well drained.' He crossed the yard and picked a leaf from one of the vines. 'These are Vilana.' He passed the leaf to Chloe. 'They're one of the most widely grown varieties on the island and are linked to the vines that were grown here in Minoan times, perhaps even before. They give a good yield and are a staple of many of the village wines you get here.'

Chloe listened keenly as her grandfather warmed to the subject. 'Before we left, I was experimenting with growing another grape I thought might blend well with the Vilana and look what I found in the bottom corner of the plot near the wall of the old winery.' Panagiotis reached into his shirt pocket and took out a leaf. 'This is Vidiano, a grape that has grown on Crete since Venetian times but was forgotten about for centuries. It's making a comeback and is used in some of the best whites produced here. Maybe you could think about reviving this line? There are probably more plants that have survived, and this one at least would be a start.'

Rarely had Chloe seen her grandfather so animated. His enthusiasm was infectious. 'Stop, Grandad, stop, I need to write these names down!' Chloe laughed. Although she was well trained in the science of viticulture, she valued her grandfather's and father's experience, and Panagiotis knew this land better than anyone.

'As it's our last evening before your father and I go home, let's have a celebratory dinner in Elounda. Then we can discuss plans and you can scribble down everything you want. But you can leave out anything you think won't work. After all, it's your land. Oh, and your father and I thought you should hang on to the car, at least until you can find a truck of your own. We phoned the car hire company who are happy for you to keep it at a good price as it is nearly the end of the season. Perhaps you could drop us at the airport tomorrow morning?'

'Of course I will, Grandad.' Chloe felt a wave of sadness wash over her at the thought of them leaving but pulled herself round, fired up by the challenge which lay ahead. If her confidence was wavering, she bolstered herself with the knowledge her father and grandfather had faith in her and that she had the support of her mother too.

Chloe spent the afternoon pacing out her land and making a rough map of the plot and a plan of the elevation, marking the changing qualities of the terrain. Panagiotis and Michalis were meanwhile deep in discussions about grape varieties that would thrive in the soil and the possibilities they provided for establishing a successful business.

As they drove towards the coast, Michalis stopped the car by the church in Epano Elounda. 'I just want to pop into the taverna and say goodbye to Alexander.'

The taverna owner was sad to hear he was leaving the next day, but Michalis assured him it would not be long before he returned. He thanked Alexander for finding Chloe a flat and asked if he would keep an eye out for her. As Michalis said goodbye, Alexander gripped his hand tight.

'*Sto kalo*,' his friend said as Michalis headed back to the car.

Down the mountain the autumn evening was cooling as they took their seats in the taverna, the darkening waters of the bay whispering just feet away. Chloe spread her map on the table and listened as the two men outlined their thoughts about the vineyard.

The idea was that she set aside some of the land to continue growing the Vilana grapes, thinning out the vines to get a better quality crop providing wine to sell to local tavernas. This would give her an income over the years that it would take to develop the business. She would also plant Vidiano grapes and possibly Thrapsathira to blend with the Vilana to develop a more premium white wine for the restaurant market and maybe even export. Chloe's head was swimming as her father then outlined ideas about planting vines to produce rosé and in the longer term a classic red.

'Slow down, Dad. How do you spell Kotsifali and Mandilari and after how long do you take them from the vats to the barrel?'

'Don't worry, I'll write this all down when I get home and send it to you by email, then you can study our ideas more closely and decide if you want to go ahead with them.'

It was ambitious, but could be progressed in clear stages. She trusted them and what they were suggesting.

'It would be stupid not to,' she said. 'I might have a degree, but Grandad has so much knowledge of this terroir and you both have a lifetime's experience of the business. An email would be great as I won't remember everything otherwise.'

'In that case we can stop talking business now and enjoy our last evening together. I think you've plenty of work to get started with.'

Her father was interrupted by the waiter putting a large plate of crab on the table. 'These were pulled from the bay this morning. I will crack them for you.'

Chloe looked out across the water. A caique lay at anchor offshore, illuminated by an almost full moon. She could see lights on the causeway out to the canal and the island of Kalydon. Entranced, she allowed herself to think that this was her home now.

Even this late in the season the taverna was busy with customers. Chloe and her father ordered a lamb dish covered in filo pastry, while Panagiotis skilfully filleted his grilled sea bass. When they had finished, watermelon, grapes and apple were brought to the table as well as raki, and they toasted the success of Chloe's vineyard.

Chapter 10

ON THE DRIVE back from the airport, Chloe felt a pang of loneliness. With her father and grandfather by her side she had been sure of her abilities. Now alone, she could feel her confidence begin to ebb. She had checked out of the hotel in Agios Nikolaos that morning and had her luggage and the bits and bobs she had bought on the back seat of the hire car ready to unload into her flat in the village.

She stemmed the leak in her self-belief by thinking of how strong her grandfather had been, starting a new life in Italy when he had been exiled from his homeland and how her father too had followed in his footsteps establishing a successful business in England. She told herself she had their strength within her and if she worked hard, she could achieve similar things. As she drove through the Gorge of Selinari she looked upwards and could see vultures gliding, weightless on the thermals above the mountains, and felt her inner power returning.

It took Chloe no time to unpack her few clothes and make up the bed. Her landlady had left a bottle of wine and a piece of cake to welcome her. It would have been easy to sit and wallow in the contentment of having her own place, but she decided to leave that pleasure for later and headed up the path towards the vineyard.

She had decided that she would start by reinstating the wall which marked the uphill boundary of the property. She was not sure how many of the stones she would find without clearing some of the vines from her neighbour's land, but thought she would see what she could do with her bare hands before deciding on the tools she might need to buy to complete the job. Walking along the perimeter that bordered the narrow road up the mountainside, she was surprised to spot something moving near the demolished wall.

She slowed her pace and, as she got closer, saw a man struggling to unearth stones from the tangle of vines. He had not yet seen her, so preoccupied was he with the task in hand. She could see his slender frame and his t-shirt drenched in sweat as he strained to pick up a rock and carry it to the base of the wall.

She stopped and watched his body tense as he lifted the stone onto the foundations.

'It looks like you're saving me a job,' Chloe said. The man looked up and his handsome features relaxed before taking on a look of consternation.

'And you are?' he asked.

'I'm Chloe, and this is my vineyard.' She introduced herself in Greek before pointing downhill from where the young man was working.

'Thanos.' He answered, not extending a hand.

Chloe smiled but her presence seemed to put him on edge.

'I'll let you get on with your work then.' Taken aback by the man's curt reaction, she turned and walked down the hill. She wondered whether he was related to Tassos or Sofia or a worker. Either way, he was rude and offhand. Although curious to discover who he was, his manner told her now was not the time to find out. He's rebuilding the wall anyway, it's one less job for me to do, she thought.

Thanos had not expected to see anyone there. He knew that the land had been returned to its owners, but they lived abroad, or so he thought. He looked up at the beautiful young woman as she walked away, tucking her long blond hair behind an ear, not looking back. He felt his chest and stomach tighten with guilt.

Since his mother had revealed the story of her childhood, he knew that his grandfather had stolen land from his neighbours. His mother was so traumatised by memories of the past that she would not go near her father's land and had offered the proceeds of its sale to him. Perhaps it would make enough for him to establish a taverna of his own. Maybe he could rent somewhere in Chora Sfakion, or even Chania. Although happy in Loutro, he felt that he had been treading water and was a drain on his parents' dwindling savings.

Thanos had come to clear out the house, perhaps give it a lick of paint, and tidy up the land as well as re-establishing its original boundary. He would have liked to have got in some help, but had little enough money as it was and his parents were only just making ends meet. But he had time, and could sleep in the house while he did the work.

He was used to long hours, working hard in a hot kitchen, driven by the desire to create the best dishes he could cook and finding satisfaction in the pleasure that gave to customers. He was not suited to relentless heavy labour and his arms and legs were already aching after less than a couple of hours.

He glanced down the mountainside. In the distance he could see the woman walking about in the burned-out winery. However hard he tried he could not shake the remorse he felt at the consequences of his grandfather's actions. He bent down and lifted another stone. He needed the money from the sale of the land, so would have to work as quickly as possible, avoiding his neighbour as much as he could.

Chloe wondered who the man was. Had he been hired to clear the land after the death of Tassos? He didn't seem to have the physique of someone used to manual work. His skin was pale, not tanned by working for hours in the open air. At first there was something about him to which she felt attracted, but his brusque manner and refusal to engage in conversation had been offputting. She resolved not to let the encounter put a dampener on her spirits though, and would keep away from him.

She took out her phone and dialled the number of a builder recommended by the estate agent. After making an appointment for him to visit the property the following week, she decided to make a start clearing the land. She had noticed a shop which sold agricultural supplies on the road into Elounda. Within the hour she had returned with a spade, saw, secateurs, shears, a pickaxe and some gloves.

A few hours later she was pleased at the small patch of ground she had managed to clear with four vines evenly spaced out and neatly pruned. As the evening drew in, she walked down the track back towards the village. She looked behind her up the hillside but could see no sign of the man working on the wall. Down the mountainside she saw the lights coming on in Elounda.

Too tired to cook, she decided to go to the taverna. Alexander greeted her warmly and several of the customers welcomed her with smiles or a friendly '*kalispera*'. She felt the weariness creep up on her and did not linger over her meal. When she had finished she caught Alexander's eye to get the bill. He waved her away, insisting that the meal was on him. Chloe tried to argue, but he was having none of it. How kind and welcoming people were; it won't be difficult to settle in here, she thought as she headed up the lane to her front door and bed.

*

Light came streaming through the windows the next morning and woke her. She had forgotten to close the shutters. Almost immediately her muscles reminded her of the work she had done the previous afternoon. Her body ached and she had to force herself out of bed. A shower helped ease the stiffness in her back and legs and by the time she had dressed and drunk a cup of coffee she was ready to face the walk up to the vineyard.

Her plan for the day was to start surveying and plotting where she intended to plant the grape varieties her grandfather had suggested. Once she had decided this she could assess the work she would need contractors to do and what she could do herself. First, though, she thought she would see what headway had been made on the drystone wall. From what she had witnessed the previous day she suspected progress would be slow. She needed the boundary established before any contractors could start work.

Chloe scanned the hillside for any movement. Seeing nothing, she crept slowly along the perimeter wall until she reached the place it joined the uphill limit of her property. Running her eye along the line where the boundary once stood, she was pleasantly surprised: the tangle of vines which had hidden the course of the foundations had been cleared and at the far end she could make out stones built up into a section of wall.

It was still early. The hillsides were silent, the sun not hot enough to inspire cicada song. Chloe stood and took in the peace. In the distance she heard the crow of a cockerel, and high up the mountain the tinkle of a goat bell. Then silence again. She began to walk along her side of the foundations, curious to get a closer look at the rebuilt wall, remembering she should clear a break between the boundary and her vines to stop the spread of potential fires and cross-infection.

A noise interrupted her thoughts. She stopped. Silence. Was she daydreaming? More alert she gingerly walked on, looking all around.

'Help!' Ahead of her she heard a man's voice, faint but growing stronger in panic as she got closer.

'My God! What have you done?'

Chloe could see the man who introduced himself as Thanos the previous day lying on the ground, his leg trapped under a large rock. He seemed to be in considerable pain and Chloe suspected his leg was broken. 'How long have you been here?'

Chloe received no answer. Thanos looked very pale and she realised from the red stained earth around his injured leg that he had lost a large amount of blood. Taking out her phone she searched for an emergency ambulance number and dialled it.

She bent down and heaved the large rock off him and he whimpered as the broken leg moved. 'The ambulance is on its way.' Chloe took off her belt and wrapped it twice around his leg above his knee in a makeshift tourniquet. Thanos screamed in agony, and Chloe was not sure if this was the right thing to do but she knew she needed to stop the bleeding and keep him conscious until the ambulance arrived. As they waited, time seemed to slow down. She held his limp hand and talked, desperate to keep him awake. He didn't answer, but through the pain written on his handsome face she thought that he was aware of her. Thanos looked drained of all colour. For a moment Chloe felt a pang of guilt that what she was feeling was more than concern.

Hearing the siren, Chloe ran towards the road alongside the perimeter wall, waving her hands and shouting to attract attention. As the paramedics took control, administering painkillers and oxygen before splinting the broken leg, she felt the adrenaline begin to drain from her body. She followed the two men as they carried the stretcher over the uneven ground to the ambulance.

With Thanos settled inside, one of the paramedics held open the door of the ambulance for Chloe and nodded. She climbed aboard.

*

It seemed hours since Thanos had been taken to the Emergency Department, thought Chloe as she sat in the waiting room at the hospital in Agios Nikolaos. But glancing at her watch she saw it had barely been half an hour since the gurney was pushed through the swing doors into the care of the medical team.

At last, a nurse appeared. 'He's gone for an x-ray. I'll let you know what will happen next when we get the results. Are you a relative?'

'No,' Chloe answered, sheepishly. 'I just found him and called the ambulance. He was working on the land next door to mine. But… I'd like to know that he's OK, if you don't mind?'

'You can wait here if you like and when we know more I'll come and tell you.' The nurse put a hand on Chloe's shoulder before returning through the swing doors.

The waiting room was warm and she felt herself begin to sweat. She told herself it was the shock of all that had happened. She wanted to leave, get some fresh air and a bottle of water, but was afraid that if she left she might miss news of Thanos' condition.

It felt like an eternity before the nurse reappeared.

'Would you like to come through? He's very groggy at the moment but we're just about to take him to theatre to operate.' The nurse led Chloe into the trauma ward holding aside a curtain. Beneath the sheet he looked small, his long hair framing his fine features on the pillow. A porter arrived at the bedside.

'He'll be in theatre some time,' the nurse said. 'I'd go and get some air.'

Chloe reached down and took Thanos' hand and felt a gentle squeeze. 'Good luck,' she whispered.

She hurried past patients, nurses and doctors smoking at the entrance to the hospital. She found a small supermarket and bought water. She knew she should eat but couldn't face food. She needed to let somebody know he was hurt. He couldn't be left alone in hospital with nobody knowing he was there. But who was he?

Chloe sat on a bench beside a children's playground. She watched as kids cycled bikes around a track, their parents looking on. She opened the bottle and took a long drink. The hospital was at the top of a hill above the town. Below were the lake and the port and the hotel she had stayed at with her father and grandfather and the square where they had met with Georgia. Why had she not thought of it before? Georgia must have contact details for the owners of the land. Maybe she could find out who the guy was?

Chloe followed a road down the hill until she got her bearings, and made her way to the square and the door of the solicitor's office. She rang the bell and was buzzed through to be met at the top of the stairs by the lawyer's secretary.

'What's the matter? You look dreadful.' Georgia rounded her desk and pulled out a chair as Chloe entered.

Once sitting down, she told Georgia about the accident that had happened to the man who had been rebuilding the wall, that she did not know who he was and was afraid that he would be left all alone in hospital.

Georgia understood her concern. 'I'll call the landowners now, and see what they know.' She looked up the number and dialled.

Sofia was in shock when she received the news. Georgia could not tell her much about his condition other than that he had broken his leg and was being operated on as they spoke.

'It's not me you have to thank, it's your neighbour. She found your son and took him to hospital.'

Georgia hung up the phone. 'That was Sofia, Tassos' daughter. Thanos is her son. She says they will come now, but it will take her and her husband six hours or so to get here. They will go straight to the hospital.'

Chloe decided she would stay until his parents arrived, before returning to the village.

*

In Loutro, Athanasios wasted no time in lending Milos his truck, but it was still afternoon by the time they headed into the foothills of the White Mountains. Usually Sofia would have told her husband to drive more slowly, but now in her mind she was urging him on round the sharp bends in the road, which wove its way through the hills towards the north of the island. Dusk was falling by the time they reached the national highway and it was dark as they sped past Rethymnon and on towards Heraklion.

Since that day at the lawyer's office, Sofia had remained adamant that she wanted nothing to do with her father's land, but Milos had promised her that he would handle everything, and Thanos had been thrilled by the news that he would receive the money from its sale. The opportunity to inherit the money, he had said, revived his dream of opening his own restaurant. Was the accident a sign that they should have stayed away after all?

Sofia was now anxious about her son's wellbeing but also the knowledge that it was a neighbour who had found him. These were the people whose lives her father had destroyed. She did not know who the woman Georgia had spoken of was, but with every mile closer they got to the hospital, her apprehension mounted.

Chapter 11

SITTING IN THE waiting room once more, Chloe anxiously awaited further news of Thanos.

'You can see him now.' The nurse stood over her. 'He's asleep, but don't be alarmed, the operation was long but it went as well as could be expected.'

She was ushered into a ward where Thanos lay. The nurse glanced at a monitor, the regular shape of the traces reassuring. She checked the level of painkiller in the intravenous drip attached to the cannula in his arm. A tear came to Chloe's eye.

'He'll be alright, love.' Seeing she was upset, the nurse wrapped a comforting arm around Chloe's shoulder.

'I'm OK, just tired and relieved.'

'I'll be in to check him regularly. In the meantime, let me know if he needs anything.'

Left alone with Thanos, Chloe settled into a chair beside the bed. She looked at his handsome face, drawn and pale, his dark hair pushed behind his ears. Beneath the crisp white sheet she could not detect the rise and fall of his chest, and put her face close to his to check he was breathing. She tried to stay awake but the heat and her tiredness got the better of her and soon she was asleep.

*

'Thano, what have you done?'

Sofia passed through the door held open for her by the nurse, followed by Milos. She stood staring at her sleeping son and tears ran down her cheeks.

Chloe, jolted awake, rubbed her eyes, got to her feet and held out a hand, introducing herself. 'You must be Sofia,' she said softly. 'I was with Georgia when she called you. Here, sit down. Would you like me to go and get you both a coffee or anything? I could do with some fresh air.'

If the young woman bore any grudges, her friendly manner showed no signs of such a grievance.

'I'd love one, thank you,' replied Sofia.

'I'd like one too if you don't mind?' said Milos.

'I won't be long, there's a café nearby.'

After establishing how Thanos' parents liked their coffee, Chloe was relieved to leave the room. She welcomed the cool night air and the feeling that she was no longer solely responsible for Thanos' wellbeing. As she waited for her takeaway drinks, though, she felt herself feeling impatient to return, a sensation that bewildered and unnerved her.

When she got back, Sofia and Milos had been brought chairs, the one she had sat on still vacant. They thanked her for the coffee and bid her sit down.

'We can't thank you enough for saving Thanos' life. The nurse has been telling me how badly injured he was. She says he should recover fine, but it will take a long time, some time in hospital, then maybe months on crutches and physiotherapy to get him walking again. Thanos was fortunate that you were around. I understand from Georgia that you own the land next door.'

'I didn't know who Thanos was until I went to Georgia's office and she rang you. I found him with his leg trapped beneath a rock, bleeding, and called the ambulance. I thought he might have been a worker fixing the wall for you. I was going to start the job myself, but he had beaten me to it.'

Sofia's face crumpled and she began to cry, overwhelmed by the image of her son injured on the mountainside, and relieved that he would be OK. 'Thank you,' was all she could mumble between sobs, burying her head on her husband's shoulder.

Chloe was silent for a moment, then thought she would clear the air. 'I am Michalis' daughter.' She could see the unease on Sofia's face and Milos grabbed his wife's hand. 'I know about what happened with the vineyard, and between you and my dad all those years ago.' Chloe tried to make light of the matter and put Sofia, who was clearly upset, at ease. 'From what my dad told me, it sounds to me that you were more the victim.'

As her tears dried, Sofia could sense the anxiety she held deep within drain from her. The young woman was right, both she and her mother had been victims of her father's abuse.

Chloe continued. 'My great-grandfather, grandfather and father all made new and happy lives for themselves, and as I said to Dad, if the fire hadn't happened he wouldn't have met my mum and had me.'

'I don't know anything about what happened after I escaped on the day of the fire,' said Sofia. 'How is Michalis? Is he well?'

Chloe happily recounted the story of her family's flight from Crete, how they established the vineyard in Italy before Michalis met her mother and moved to England. How her family had all but forgotten about the land in the village until they had got the call from Georgia out of the blue. That was when – only recently – her father had told her the whole story. Chloe went on to say that she had fallen in love with the island and intended to rebuild the winery and house and replant the land, running it as a business.

Hearing Chloe's words, Sofia found comfort in the knowledge that the young woman who had saved her son's life bore no grudges against her family, and she in turn felt able to open up about the past; how Tassos had imprisoned her after seeing her with Michalis and set fire to the land, as her mother had told her; how she and her mother had fled to Loutro and then made a new life in Athens, before losing almost everything in the ongoing financial crisis and returning to Crete. Sofia admitted to wanting nothing to do with her cruel father's land but saw the wisdom in selling it to help her son forge a future. She looked at Thanos and a tear came to her eye. If she hadn't offered the land to him, he would not have been hurt.

'It was an accident. Your son is a grown man. You must not blame yourself,' Chloe reassured Sofia.

'You have been so kind and you must want to get home, you are tired. Milos will drive you.' Sofia looked at her husband.

'No, I'll be fine. I had a sleep in the chair before you arrived,' said Chloe.

Something held her at the bedside of this young man who she hardly knew but now felt an attachment to. Had she really saved his life as Sofia had said? She had not given herself time to think about that. She had done what most people would have in that situation.

'I hope I'm not imposing by staying. It's just… I feel I have to know that he's OK.'

Sofia reached out for the young woman's hand. 'You're not intruding in any way. We owe you everything.'

As evening fell into night, they sat around the bed in companionable silence, grabbing moments of sleep under the dimmed hospital lights. It was three in the morning when Thanos stirred.

Emerging from the dark nothingness, he struggled to grasp where he was. His mouth was parched. He moved his head and saw his mother and father asleep. Something touched his hand. With effort he turned his head the other way. Blinking, he saw the beautiful young woman who was now holding his hand. It stirred something in his memory. He struggled to raise his head off the pillow and caught sight of his plastered leg.

'You're in hospital,' Chloe said.

Milos jumped up, followed by Sofia. 'Thank God, you're awake.'

'I'll get a nurse.' Chloe left the room.

'My throat, it's so dry,' Thanos whispered and his father poured water from a jug into a plastic cup and held it to his lips.

Chloe returned with a nurse who efficiently took readings from the monitor and checked the intravenous fluids before writing on the charts at the end of the bed. 'Everything is as we'd expect, you'll feel a bit drowsy for a while,' the nurse said to Thanos before turning to his parents. 'He's on a high dose of medication to manage the pain. Give him a drink when he wants one. I'll be in and out to check up on him and a doctor will be round in the morning.'

She left the room and Thanos closed his eyes. Now the darkness was replaced by flashes of what had happened. Intent on getting the land ready for sale, he had got up before dawn, starting work on the wall early to avoid the awkwardness of encountering his neighbour. He was lifting a heavy rock, then stumbled, the stone crushing his leg. In agony, he used his last drops of energy to cry for help. Then there was nothing but darkness... He opened his eyes again. The woman who had introduced herself to him as Chloe was asleep in the chair at his bedside. Why was she here, when he had been so rude to her?

Slowly, through the fog of his memory he remembered calling out, and her being there... In some way the acute embarrassment which he felt at meeting Chloe again far outweighed the pain in his leg.

He turned his head away from her, and his mother brought the cup of water to his lips. It was lukewarm but welcome. He mouthed a thank you and fell back into a deep sleep.

The night wore on, punctuated by the comings and goings of the nurse and the fitful sleep of those keeping vigil. As light began to seep through the blinds, Thanos heard himself moan, and in that moment of consciousness felt the pain in his broken leg. Sofia went out to find a nurse who brought more pain relief. The analgesic which was administered worked quickly and the pain ebbed.

Checking with the nurse that it was OK for him to eat, Chloe offered to go and get him breakfast if she could find a store open that early. She made her way out through the already busy hospital corridors and walked the way she knew towards the square. The early morning air was warm and fresh with the prospect of a beautiful day. Baskets of fruit were being arranged outside a greengrocer's and a fishmonger hosed down the floor in his shop. People wished her '*kalimera*' as she walked by. She stopped at a cash machine and withdrew money from her account, then found a minimarket and bought a selection of yoghurts and pastries.

On her walk back to the hospital, her mind turned to the day ahead. She supposed she should get a bus back to Elounda, walk up the donkey track to the village and continue work at the vineyard. But she felt a strange reluctance to leave Thanos' bedside, which was ridiculous, she thought: she had only just met the man, and when she had, he hadn't been at all friendly. When she found him injured, she had simply done what she could and called for an ambulance. Now she had to get back to her land and get on with her life and her original plan of rebuilding the wall. That would help Thanos too. She made up her mind that after she had some breakfast she would get back to Elounda and resume the schedule she had planned.

Inside the hospital she made her way through the corridors to the recovery ward. Then she stopped. There were raised voices inside the room. Should she go in? Hesitating outside, she heard the voice of Thanos, weak but stubborn, arguing with his parents.

'You cannot afford to stay in a hotel in Agios Nikolaos all the time I am stuck in here, and anyway, Athanasios will need his truck for the farm.' Thanos was insistent.

'I can return the truck and make my way back by bus whilst your mother stays here,' said Milos.

'I will be fine,' said Thanos firmly.

'It will be as cheap for us to stay here and look after you as to pay for a nurse to care for you,' argued Sofia, though she knew they would struggle to pay for either. They had suspended their health insurance when they had gone out of business in Athens.

'I'm sorry, I couldn't help overhearing,' Chloe said as she entered the room, putting the bag of shopping on the bed. 'I could look after him.'

The room went silent. What was she thinking? Chloe did not know what had made her come out with the shock interjection. And yet it did make sense. 'I live much closer than you and have a hire car. I suspect he will not be in here much longer than a week or so as they'll be needing the bed. Then you can come and take him home to Loutro.'

'We couldn't possibly let you do that,' Sofia said, looking at her husband.

'Of course not,' Milos agreed.

Thanos, listening, couldn't imagine being cared for by someone whom he had just met, particularly considering the history of their two families, but on the other hand he knew his parents could not afford to pay for the nursing care he would need whilst he was in hospital. He was torn.

The more Sofia and Milos put up objections, the more adamant Chloe became. Thanos saw the determination in the young woman's deep blue eyes and heard the kindness in her soft but resolute voice.

'If she doesn't mind?' Thanos looked enquiringly at Chloe. 'It won't be for long, and then Dad can come to pick me up.'

His parents could see that they were fighting a losing battle.

'Thank you for your kindness,' said Sofia. 'We don't deserve this.'

'It really is nothing. I'm happy to do it. If you don't mind, before you go I'd like to return home and pack a few bits and get my car.'

'I'll take you,' insisted Milos, 'and maybe we can pick up Thanos some clothes and washing stuff from the house.'

On the drive Milos asked Chloe about her plans for the vineyard and how she felt about moving to a new country even though she was half Greek. She told him how comfortable she felt being in Crete and explained how she had studied viniculture at university and hoped to make a success of her fledgling business.

Back at her flat, Chloe washed and changed. She then returned to where she had left her car and where Milos was waiting in the van, and followed him up the road to Tassos' old house. Entering the building where the old man had been found dead, she saw that Thanos would have his work cut out returning it to a habitable state. The rendering was flaking and old newspapers stuffed into cracks in the nicotine-stained walls, bare wood was showing through the cracked blue paint on the doors, window frames and shutters, cobwebs hung from every corner in every room. A rusty bed frame sat on sticky linoleum littered with old bottles.

Milos opened the door to the back bedroom. The window was boarded up with wood nailed to the crumbling frame. This must have been where his wife had been locked in before the fire. He shuddered and closed the door. Finding the room where his son had been sleeping, he hunted for some clean clothes. He found a toothbrush and toothpaste on the basin in the primitive bathroom. Milos understood how Sofia would want nothing to do with this place. Even for him, who had never been there before, it conjured up horrific thoughts of the trauma his wife and her mother must have suffered at the hands of Tassos.

Both Chloe and Milos were relieved when they closed the door on the house. They stopped for a moment and looked over the tangle of vines down to Chloe's vineyard and the burned-out shell of the buildings there, to the olive groves and village beyond and in the distance the bay. The view lifted their spirits as they returned to their respective vehicles. Alone with his thoughts, as he drove back towards the hospital Milos thought how generous it was of Chloe to offer to look after his son. He could not pretend that he wasn't relieved. Money was tight for himself and Sofia. Even staying for a week in a hotel would have caused them considerable financial hardship. Hiring a nurse would have been even more expensive. But Chloe's generosity still amazed him when he thought of how the actions of his wife's father had destroyed her family's life in Crete.

Following behind Milos, Chloe was still bemused by her offer to care for Thanos. It had come out of the blue, but she had no regrets. There was something which drew her to him; despite being a few years older than her, he seemed like a lost soul. In contrast to his abrupt manner when they had first met, she could see a kindness in his dark brown eyes and heard the gentleness in his voice. She had also witnessed the concern he had for his parents' wellbeing. Looking after him would not be for long, and then his parents could return and take him back to Loutro to convalesce.

Sofia was crying as she got into the truck alongside her husband.

Chloe reached through the open passenger window and hugged her. 'Don't worry, I'll look after him. Give me a ring when you get home and I'll give you an update on how he is progressing,' said Chloe through the passenger window.

Sofia blew Chloe a kiss as they drove away. Chloe turned and walked back inside the hospital.

Chapter 12

BEING ALONE WITH her for the first time since he had regained consciousness, Thanos felt awkward. He told himself that her caring for him was no different from a nurse. But there was something about the connection between them that made this very different.

Chloe could see that Thanos was uncomfortable and was careful not to discomfit her patient, while Thanos in turn was determined to spare her dealing with his more intimate needs and that spurred him on to do as much as he could for himself. He insisted on washing himself and Chloe would discreetly draw the curtain.

They got into a routine of Chloe arriving early in the morning and staying throughout the day. She brought his meals, but otherwise the days passed slowly. Each afternoon Chloe would phone Sofia and tell her of the progress her son was making, before passing her phone to Thanos so that he could chat with his mother.

During the long days, when he wasn't dozing, they would talk about their plans for the land they had each inherited. Chloe related to Thanos how she had been utterly captivated by Crete and how she intended to restore the vineyard. He told her that he too adored the island where they had only recently moved from Athens. He spoke of the demonstrations against austerity in the capital and the shock he had first felt when his parents had to close their restaurant and the family had had to leave everything they had worked so hard for behind. Thanos explained how he wanted to sell his land as soon as possible to raise money to establish his own taverna.

There was something in Chloe's tenacity to make a success of her venture which he found inspirational and gave him more of a sense of purpose. He opened up to her about his love for cooking with only the freshest produce which was local and in season. When he talked about his ambition his eyes sparkled, revealing the passion in him.

Alone at home in the evenings, keen to plough on with work, Chloe drew a map of the land, marking on it details of the vine variety, number of plants, soil quality, drainage and irrigation. She compiled a detailed to-do list for herself and for the builders who were contracted to start on the tumbledown buildings in January.

She spoke to her father regularly on the phone, and told him about Thanos being in hospital. At first he was disconcerted that Chloe had met Sofia, but relaxed a bit when his daughter reassured him how kind she was. Chloe kept quiet about the fact that she was going every day to nurse Thanos. He seemed happy enough with the progress she was making with the vineyard, and she was content to leave things at that.

So resolute was Thanos to get up and about and out of the hospital that he worked hard with the physiotherapist and with Chloe's help impressed the doctors with his progress. Ten days after the accident they deemed him fit to leave and he called his father to make the long drive to come and take him home.

There was real affection in the hug Thanos gave Chloe before he was helped into the truck. Chloe was touched by the box of sweet pastries Sofia had made and handed her as a gesture of thanks for her kindness. As they drove out of the hospital car park, Chloe was surprised by the pang of despondency she felt at Thanos' departure. She tried to shake it, but it lingered as she drove out of the town. The view of the Bay of Korfos from the top of the mountain between Agios Nikolaos and Elounda usually made her happy, but even that failed to relieve the strange loss she felt at his leaving.

Over the next few weeks Chloe threw herself into rebuilding the wall. With each rock she heaved into place she felt she was helping the man with whom, if she was honest with herself, she was falling in love.

*

Even in the late autumn days, Chloe found herself sweating with the heavy lifting. At night she returned to her flat drained. In the mornings her whole body ached. After showering, the walk up the track to her land helped ease the stiffness in her bones as she embarked on another day carefully selecting rocks and hefting them into place to build the wall. Scorpions and the occasional lizard scuttled out from beneath the stones and she was pleased that she was wearing gloves to protect her hands. Progress was painfully slow as she needed to catch her breath after lifting each rock. But despite the soreness in her body, she found the work satisfying.

She kept her father updated with the progress she was making: that the builders would be starting in the New Year, and that meanwhile she had completed the first layer of the wall. She joked about it getting easier as she built higher as the stones needed were smaller and she wouldn't have to bend down as far.

She knew that her dad was right, however, when he suggested that now the boundary was at least clearly marked, she should leave that for the moment and turn her attention to the land. That involved selecting the vines she wanted to keep, erecting the posts and wires to create the trellises and clearing the earth between the rows. It was crucial that she have this work completed by springtime, when she would need to plant the new stock and varieties of grape or their business plan would be set back a year.

She resolved to start work on the land; she could go back to building the wall at any time. She had marked out the extent of her property anyway, so why was she so keen to finish the job now? She had not heard anything of Thanos, and didn't know when, or if, he would return.

Some evenings she would go to eat in the taverna. Alexander was always interested to know how she was progressing and many of the other customers were not shy to ask what she was doing on the land. She felt welcome in the village, her neighbours greeting her whenever she walked past them in the lanes.

It was late November when she put her tools in a wheelbarrow and pushed it to the top of the vineyard. Using wooden pegs and string, she transferred the detail from her plan to the land, working methodically downhill. After that first day's work she had managed to mark out where the rows of vines should go and in which direction. Somehow the simple process of hammering in the stakes and stringing lines between them made the work which lay ahead seem more manageable. But she knew from experience that selecting the strong vines she wanted to keep and moving them to replace the dead or weaker ones, as well as constructing trellises and clearing the spaces between, was a mammoth task.

It was nearly Christmas by the time she had determined the strongest vines, which she carefully dug up and moved into the rows she had demarcated. With a scythe she then began to cut back the jungle of weeds and unwanted vines between the lines where she intended to hammer in the posts and string out the wires to support the plants she would keep. She was grateful that the weather had turned cooler, but as the evening began to draw in at the end of that first day of backbreaking work, she stood and surveyed her progress. She had not even completed clearing one row. At this rate it would take her forever to get the ground ready for spring unless she could employ some help. The money her father and grandfather had given her, though, had already been earmarked for the builders.

There was nothing else for it but to phone her father and ask his advice.

Her father was unfazed. 'Your grandfather and I knew that would be only the first tranche of investment you will need. I'm more worried that you sound a bit down,' Michalis said. 'I hope you're not working too hard and wearing yourself out.'

'Do I? I don't mean to. I am working hard, but I enjoy it,' replied Chloe.

'Why don't you come home for a few days over Christmas? Your mother would love to see you, and so would I. I can book you tickets. Would you like to come?'

'I'd love to.' Chloe didn't hesitate. Suddenly, she realised she was missing home. The loneliness had crept up on her stealthily. Since Thanos had left hospital to return to Loutro she thought she had been content on her own, working all hours on the land. Until that moment as she was speaking with her father, she had not realised that something was missing.

'I'll get online right away and see what I can find, I'll call you back later,' promised her father.

As she hung up, Chloe reflected on what had happened. She had not given returning to England over Christmas a thought, but now it was likely to happen she felt her spirits rise. Perhaps she could do with a break. She brushed away the thought that she might be missing Thanos. She hardly knew him. Nursing him in hospital had just been an act of kindness towards someone in need, so why did she feel his absence so deeply? Perhaps she was just feeling a bit isolated and nostalgic at this time of year. A trip home to see Mum and Dad would surely recharge her batteries.

Her father managed to book flights to Heathrow via Athens on Christmas Eve, returning on New Year's Day. Chloe already felt her mood lift at the prospect, and with renewed vigour set about finding a contractor to help clear the land. If anything, the imposed deadline of leaving for Christmas spurred her on. The day before her departure she had in place a company to take on the ground works alongside the builders.

Chapter 13

IT WAS EARLY evening by the time the plane touched down in London. With only hand luggage, Chloe breezed through arrivals and rushed towards her waiting father, hugging him tightly.

'Let's get you home, your mother can't wait to see you.' Michalis took her bag and set off towards the car park.

The windscreen wipers pushed aside the drizzle. On the motorway the lights of lorries and cars of last-minute travellers returning home for Christmas contrasted starkly with the seclusion of her life on Crete. She loved Christmas Eve, the wonderful anticipation of the celebration to come as cheering as the big day itself. In the rain and speeding traffic, Michalis had to concentrate hard. The radio played familiar Christmas songs and Chloe made light conversation about her journey while her father drove towards the country lanes which would lead them home.

As her father swung the car into the gravelled driveway, Chloe felt a glow inside at the illuminated reindeer on the lawn and the wreath on the door as it was opened by her mum. Tess, the family's black Labrador rushed towards her, jumping up and licking her face. Mother and daughter hugged each other tightly.

'Welcome home, darling. We've missed you. Come in and get something to drink and some food.' Holding her daughter's hand, Charlotte led her inside. Chloe was delighted to see the usual Christmas Eve spread: a roast ham, cheeses, pickles, pies and sandwiches. Her father twisted the cork on a bottle of sparkling wine and poured three glasses. 'It's good to have you back. Here's to a very happy Christmas.'

The wine was cold but Chloe could not have felt warmer inside. By the window stood the tree, where it had always been placed every Christmas that she could remember. Beneath it lay a few scattered presents. She walked over and searched for the red glass bauble with her name on which her parents had bought the year she was born. It hung in pride of place right at the front of the tree. She bent down and patted Tess, who would not leave her side – they had missed each other. Across the room her father put another log on the fire blazing in the grate.

'Grab a plate. You must be starving.' Charlotte gestured towards the table. 'Carve some ham, Miki, and cut the pie or we'll never get started.'

Over supper her parents wanted to know about Thanos' accident. Chloe, reluctant to say she had stayed at his bedside, she said that as far as she knew he had gone back to Loutro. She was pleased when talk moved on to the vineyard. They chatted about yields, blending and plans for when each proposed vintage would be ready for market.

The conversation turned to the house and winery. Chloe let them know the builders were optimistic about the state the buildings. Although the roofs had collapsed, behind the plants and shrubs that had taken up residence in the ruins, the walls remained solid as she had first thought. Once the vegetation had been cleared it was hoped that, with new roofs, windows and doors, the walls could be re-rendered and the buildings would be watertight ready for new electrics and plumbing. Talking about the project that Christmas Eve, it seemed less daunting than when she was alone in Crete.

'Shall we sit on some more comfy chairs?' Charlotte stood and walked over to one of the two large sofas by the fire.

Picking up their glasses, Michalis and Chloe followed. In the warmth, sinking into the soft cushions, Chloe struggled to keep her eyes open.

'Before you go back, let me see the quotes for the work and I'll transfer some more money into the business account.' Michalis could see the gratitude on his daughter's face. 'We need to get up and running as soon as possible, then we will see a return on all of our investments sooner. Also I have a surprise for you. We want you to buy a truck, a Christmas present from your mother and me. Renting a car is expensive and it's not practical as a work vehicle. As soon as you go back I've asked Georgia if she will go with you to sort out the paperwork on a suitable 4x4. Happy Christmas, darling.'

'Thank you. I don't know what to say. And I only had time to pick you up a few bits at the Duty Free shop at the airport! Oh, that reminds me, have you any spare wrapping paper I can have?'

'I'm sure we can find some,' said Charlotte, and she laughed as Chloe hugged each parent in turn and gave them a kiss. Back in her childhood home celebrating a family Christmas, it was hard to think about the vineyard and everything she faced to make her dream a reality; but with her parents' faith in her, all worries about the business drained away.

'I'm tired. I really should go to bed. Mum, can I have that wrapping paper and some tape?'

Upstairs, Chloe felt the comforting familiarity of her bedroom. She looked out the window and laughed to herself at the reindeer, its lights flickering through the rain. She sat down and started to wrap the presents she had bought for her parents; a box of baklava each, a bottle of raki for Dad and some perfume for Mum. It seemed so little when she thought of all they had done for her. She heard a knock. 'Wait a second.' Hastily she pushed the presents under the bed. 'It's OK now, you can come in.'

Charlotte opened the door. 'I just wanted to say goodnight and tell you how proud we are of you.'

'I love you Mum, but you and Dad have been so generous.'

'Isn't that what parents do if they can? Anyway, the way I see it, it's you who are being generous. I have never seen your father so happy. Deep down, for all these years I think he blamed himself for losing the vineyard. Now the family has reclaimed it and you are bringing the land back to life. And, as he says, it's an investment. Goodnight, darling. Happy Christmas.'

'Happy Christmas, Mum.'

Charlotte closed the door softly and Chloe retrieved the half-wrapped presents from beneath her bed. She allowed her thoughts to drift back to Crete and wondered how Thanos was. She was being foolish. Had her neighbour shown her anything more than gratitude for looking after him? She didn't even know if she would ever see him again. With some effort she pushed the thought aside and finished her wrapping. Opening the door, she crept downstairs and put the presents under the twinkling tree. She smiled to see a stocking hung from the mantelpiece above the glowing embers of the fire.

Christmas day dawned cold and fresh and the weak sunshine which had banished the overnight rain sneaked in behind the heavy curtains. Chloe awoke from the soundest of sleeps. Below she could hear the soft conversation of her parents. She went downstairs to the kitchen where her mother was preparing breakfast whilst her father was peeling potatoes in readiness for Christmas lunch. Already she could smell the turkey slowly roasting in the oven.

'Happy Christmas!' Chloe greeted her parents.

'Happy Christmas!' they replied in chorus.

'We thought we'd let you sleep after your long journey yesterday,' said Charlotte. 'I'm about to do some scrambled egg and smoked salmon. Would you like some?'

'Sounds delicious. Have I got time for a quick shower first?' asked Chloe.

'Of course, there's no rush. We're just about to have a Buck's fizz, I'll pour you one for when you come down.'

After showering, Chloe dressed in a t-shirt and jeans and searched in her wardrobe for a Christmas jumper. Back downstairs, whilst her mother cooked breakfast, she delved into the stocking which had been hanging from the mantelpiece. She smiled at the gifts, some chocolates, a pound coin, a satsuma and a hospitality apron printed with a picture of a bunch of grapes. Chloe raised her glass 'Cheers, thank you, Happy Christmas, *yammas*!'

Breakfast over, Michalis returned to his preparations for lunch. 'Why don't you two head out for a walk with Tess while I finish off here? I'll catch you up in a bit. Then we can come home and open some presents.'

Outside the winter sun was low in the clear, thin blue sky. Mother and daughter walked to the back of the house, passing through the five-bar gate which led to the vineyard. In front of them acres of vines spread in neatly pruned rows. Chloe thought of her vineyard back in the village. How much work she would have to do to before her land resembled anything like this.

Reading her daughter's thoughts, her mother took her hand. 'It takes a lot of time and love to make a vineyard, and longer still to make good wine. This took my parents and your father and me years to achieve. You'll get there too. Be patient.'

The ground was soft underfoot after the overnight rain and they heard the squelch of Michalis' boots as he approached, joining his wife and daughter as they walked downhill through the pruned vines. Chloe thought about her mother's words. As they reached the hedged boundary of the property and looked back up the hill towards the house she felt pride in what her parents had achieved, and a new sense of determination that she could make a success of the vineyard in Crete.

Back inside, Michalis lit the fire and, with the delicious smells of lunch roasting in the oven, they sat down to open their presents: books and CDs which Chloe could fit in her case, and the last-minute gifts she had brought for her parents from Crete.

Michalis stood and went to the oven to check the turkey before taking a bottle of wine from the fridge and pouring them some drinks.

'We have another gift for you.' Michalis stooped behind the Christmas tree, and handed Chloe a small package. She turned over the tag on the present and looked enquiringly at her parents as she read 'Happy Christmas, with lots of love from Maria. x'.

'It was your great-grandmother's. Panagiotis and Calliope wanted you to have it,' said Charlotte.

Chloe carefully removed the wrapping, revealing a green box. She opened the lid and took out a gold bracelet, the band entwined with silver vines and bunches of grapes fashioned from pearls.

'It's beautiful,' whispered Chloe.

'Apparently Christos bought it for Maria and gave it to her on their wedding day. They would have been so proud that you are restoring the vineyard he worked so hard to establish after the war.' Charlotte crossed the room and gently lifted the gift from the padded box and fixed it around her daughter's wrist.

Chloe felt tears come to her eyes, which she couldn't take off the stunning bracelet. 'Thank you.' She kissed her mother and stood and kissed her father before blowing a kiss heavenwards. 'And thank you too.'

'It's almost time for lunch, I think,' said Michalis, standing, wary of the emotion of the moment. 'I'll just finish off the last bits and pieces.'

'Have I got time to ring Granny and Grandad to thank them for the bracelet and wish them a Happy Christmas?' asked Chloe.

'Of course, we'll be a few minutes yet,' replied her father.

*

In Loutro, as Christmas had approached, Thanos had been impatient to get back on his feet. He was up and about on his crutches but the doctors had told him it would be another month at least before the plaster could come off. He was frustrated that he could not get on with preparing his late grandfather's house for sale, in order to progress with his ideas for setting up his own taverna.

If he was honest with himself, there was another reason he wanted to get the whole business over and done with: Chloe. From the first time he had seen the young woman he had been attracted to her. Initially he had felt awkward about the consequences his grandfather's actions had had on her family's lives. Despite that, she had saved his life and nursed him in hospital.

Any relationship he formed with Chloe was bound to end in heartbreak. He lived so far away and was bent on helping support his parents in their retirement, and still felt a lingering shame about his family's past. It was best to avoid even thinking about her. With time on his hands, that was easier said than done. He needed something to keep him occupied. He felt remorse at his decision to keep away from her, but it was for the best. There was nevertheless no escaping the fact that he would need to clean up the property and sell it to move his plans forward.

As he slowly made his way on his crutches through the narrow alleyways of Loutro, Thanos took little joy from the decorated models of boats he could see through windows, or the caiques strung with Christmas lights in the harbour. He seemed to have lost his taste for the sugary almond *kourabiedes* biscuits, and the melting cinnamon-and-honey *melomakarona* cookies his mother served fresh from the oven. He was little cheered by the children singing carols on Christmas Eve. His mother urged him to ring Chloe and wish her a Happy Christmas but he was too embarrassed to make the call.

Even the traditional lamb roast on Christmas Day, a feast shared with Despina and Athanasios, had lost its flavour, and Thanos sat picking at the food on his plate. Sofia and Milos could sense their son's disquiet and decided to try and talk through his unhappiness. Seeing his parents were worried, he admitted that since the accident he felt life had been standing still and he was upset not to be able to sell the property they had given him and move on with his plans.

As Sofia and Milos washed the dishes they discussed their son's predicament. They hated seeing him unhappy. At first Sofia had thought that giving him her inheritance might atone for the guilt she felt at the loss of the taverna in Athens, but it appeared that the well-intentioned gift had caused Thanos nothing but trouble.

'It's bad luck, that's all,' said Milos. 'As soon as he gets back on his feet and gets rid of it he'll be able to move forward.'

Sofia looked unconvinced.

Milos thought for a while and then said, 'Look, why don't I go to the village with him and finish building the wall and clean up the house a bit, then I can phone Georgia and get the sale in motion. It won't fetch as much as if we had time to renovate the place and tidy up the land, but it will get it out of our lives and should give Thanos enough cash to start his business.'

Sofia seemed pleased at the idea. 'I'm happy for you to do that, Milo; anything that might cheer him up. Why don't you ask him?'

When they rejoined Thanos, Despina and Athanasios at the table, Milos put the suggestion to his son.

Thanos' smile lit up his dark eyes. 'Thanks, Papa, that would be amazing. When can we go?'

Sofia, pleased to see her son more motivated, gave them her blessing to leave the following day, hoping they could finish the work by New Year's Eve.

Athanasios was happy to lend them his truck, as always, but pointed out that there would be no ferry to Chora Sfakion the following day and there was no way that Thanos on crutches could walk the precarious cliff path there. 'Leave it with me, and I'll see what I can organise.'

He excused himself and left the house, returning half an hour later. One of the waiters from the taverna had agreed to take Milos and Thanos to Chora Sfakion in Athanasios' fishing boat early the following morning, while he went up the mountain to get his truck, meeting them there and returning with the waiter to Loutro. With the roads empty for the holiday, Milos and Thanos should be able to get to Epano Elounda by early afternoon.

*

The dawn broke bright and the sea was like a mirror as the caique cut a course to Chora Sfakion. From there they drove north through the foothills of the White Mountains, where the villages were deserted. As they turned eastwards along the national highway they caught glimpses of the sea stretching away to where it met the clearest of skies. If there was one cloud on the horizon, it was that Thanos might bump into Chloe. He was hoping that with it being Christmas, she might not be working on her land.

By afternoon they were driving through Elounda and up the mountain road, past the village then Chloe's vineyard, before pulling up outside Tassos' old house. Milos was tired after the long drive. Although the house was as uninviting as he remembered it, he suggested they both rest before walking down to the wall and reminding themselves of the work that needed to be started the following morning.

Thanos insisted his father sleep on the bed he had made up before his accident. He cleared some old newspapers off the single chair in the living space and tried to rest there, dozing fitfully, his father snoring in the bedroom. A couple of hours later he awoke and they set off down the hill to assess the situation. Thanos could not remember what he had managed to build on the day of his accident, and was sure it wasn't much. But it was immediately clear that more had been done. His father led the way along the boundary and stopped, looking down on a patch of earth stained with blood. This was where the boulder must have crushed Thanos' leg. But there was no sign of the fallen rock and the wall was built up to almost knee height.

'Someone's been working hard,' remarked Milos.

Thanos wondered if Chloe could have done all this and if she was around.

His father said, 'Well, tell you what, I'll continue with this tomorrow while you start on clearing up the house, whatever you can manage. I don't envy you that task.'

Thanos was relieved, however, to stay in the house the following morning as it meant less chance of encountering Chloe. He spent the day filling rubbish sacks with the detritus which littered the place. On his crutches progress was slow, but he was intent on contributing as much as he could to getting the house ready for sale. The more he cleared, the more was revealed that needed doing to make it fetch a good price. Beneath the grime the wooden window frames were rotten and the walls cracked, the floors uneven and stained. He would just have to clean it up as best he could in the few days he was there and hope that they could find a buyer willing to do the rest.

He steeled himself and opened the door to the back bedroom where his mother had been held captive as a child. He felt a shudder pass through him. The house had brought nothing but bad luck to his family, first to his mother and grandmother, and then to him. A picture of Chloe sitting by his bedside in hospital flashed through his head. He tried to push it away. He was fixed in his resolve to make a new life for himself near his parents in Loutro and get rid of this place fast.

Thanos knocked out the board in the window. Letting in light and air did little to lift the overriding oppression in the room. He worked as quickly as he was able, discarding everything he could into a rubbish bag before sweeping up and leaving the room, shutting the door behind him. He went outside and nailed the board back over the window.

Milos worked on the wall for three more days, while Thanos swept and mopped the floors and washed the mouldy walls and windows. It was exhausting work on his crutches and however hard he tried, he could not remove the appalling aura of the house's past. He was relieved when his father announced that the wall was finished and once he had appointed a local estate agent to handle the sale the following morning they could leave.

That New Year's Eve, as they set off down the mountainside, Milos could sense his son relax, as though a weight had been lifted from his soul. Climbing the hill leading out of Elounda, the young man did not even look back at the bay burnished by the milky morning sun. As they put the miles between them and the village, Thanos began to open up about the taverna he hoped to establish, and how in the New Year he resolved to make that dream come true.

Chapter 14

CHLOE WAS SAD to be leaving her parents, but as her father drove her through the pouring rain to Heathrow she was eager to get back to the vineyard. Reinvigorated after Christmas, and with the prospect of the work about to start on the buildings and the land, as well as the added bonus of buying a truck, she looked forward to what lay ahead. She wasn't sorry to leave the rain behind and checked the weather forecast for Crete on her phone, grateful to see that it was dry and sunny. She smiled at the thought of being outside in the fresh air during the day, and cosy in the evening by the log fire she hoped to light in the grate in her apartment.

It was dark by the time she landed in Heraklion, but she could still smell the tang of mountain herbs lingering in the air.

Picking up her car from the car park and setting off eastwards, she had a feeling of belonging. As she neared Elounda and crested the mountain above the bay, her heart lifted at the sight of the lights of the town twinkling beside the dark waters.

She continued up to the village and parked beside the church. Epano Elounda lay in darkness, most of the inhabited dwellings shuttered in against the cold of the winter evening. She was hungry but a walk to the taverna confirmed what she had suspected, it was closed. She had some crisps and biscuits in the cupboard at the flat which would have to do until morning as she was too tired to drive back down to town.

Chloe awoke refreshed; her sleep had been dreamless. It was still dark, and she checked her phone: after seven, it would be light soon. It was Friday and the workers would not begin until Monday so she was keen to get outside and watch the sunrise. She dressed in her jeans, t-shirt and jumper, grabbed her coat and headed out of the village up the path through the olive groves towards the vineyard. The sky emerged clear from the darkness, but a cold wind blew down the mountain to the sea. Chloe pulled her coat tight around her. She looked at the bay and to the east where, at the foot of the shadowy mountains, a fiery sun glowed orange as it rose above the horizon. Her heart lifted at the sight of the vines, wild and as yet untended but so full of potential.

Skirting the perimeter wall, she walked further up the mountain. Approaching the uphill border of her property, she stopped. The wall which had been less than knee high was now complete. For a moment she felt her heart flutter. Surely Thanos could not be back on his feet and have returned from Loutro? She told herself that this was impossible, but felt herself drawn towards his house.

No light came from the building and she saw no truck outside. The windows were shuttered, the gate closed. Then she caught sight of a sign roughly nailed to the peeling front door. Her heart sank as she read 'For Sale' and the phone number of an estate agent.

Turning away, she began to walk down the hill. Why was she so astonished that the place was up for sale? That had always been Thanos' intention. He had told her when he was in hospital that he wanted the proceeds to fulfil his dream and open a taverna. Whatever had she been thinking? He had never given her reason to believe that there was anything between them, so why did she feel so crestfallen at the notion that she might never set eyes on him again?

Looking down at her own land and the tangle of vines and the tumbledown buildings, she was reminded of the extent of the work awaiting her. She quickened her step. She had no time for a relationship. It was just as well Thanos had moved away and out of her life. Pushing aside the thought of him again was easier said than done, however. She tried to busy herself on the vineyard in readiness for the following week's work. But there was little she could do until the plot had been thinned, the earth rotavated and the new trellises constructed.

She fumbled in her jacket pocket for her notebook. Perhaps she could source the new grape varieties her grandfather suggested she experiment with. She had decided to test Mandilari and Kotsifali grapes as a basis for red and rosé blends. She had scribbled down the name Vidiano, the vine her grandfather had been growing to blend with the rampant Vilana grapes to produce a more sophisticated white along with the Thrapsathira variety. She remembered him showing her the leaf he had found of a plant which survived the fire.

At the lower end of the overgrown vineyard she began searching for the rogue plant. Painstakingly she pushed aside the Vilana vines, hoping to catch a glimpse of a leaf like the one Panagiotis had shown her. The search was like looking for a needle in a haystack, but at least it took her mind off Thanos.

The winter wind had calmed and the sun warmed the air so Chloe unzipped her jacket, laying it on the threshold of the winery. Something caught her eye, right near the wall of the old building. Set apart from the other vines, somehow the plant had evaded their encroachment, clinging on to its existence for all those years. It was a Vidiano! Getting up close, Chloe examined the vine, amazed at how healthy it was.

She set about digging a trench, close to where she had discovered the plant. Driving to the agricultural suppliers she bought rooting compost and several sacks of organic manure which on her return she dug into the prepared ground. With her secateurs she took cuttings from two of the healthiest shoots. Removing the soft tip growth, she snipped them into nine-inch lengths and planted them in rooting compost, and watered them in. Carefully digging around the roots of the mother plant, she moved it into the new bed alongside the hardwood cuttings.

It was late afternoon by the time she stood back and surveyed her work. From the single surviving plant, she had now got six cuttings, which she hoped would thrive there. Of course she would have to source many more to make them commercially viable, but somehow these cuttings were a symbol of her great-grandfather, grandfather and father's legacy.

The evening was already starting to draw in. Looking down the mountainside she could see lights beginning to go on in Elounda. Chloe realised that she had not eaten. She set off down the track to the village, but the taverna was again closed. Continuing downhill, she followed the village street as it turned into the cobbled donkey track which wound its way through the olive groves before emerging in the back streets of Elounda. A bell chimed, and Chloe looked up at the illuminated tower of the church near the harbour. She made her way to the waterfront and the fishing boats, Christmas lights strung from their rigging.

She found a supermarket that was open and bought some supplies to take home. Then the warm orange glow from a taverna enticed her inside where she embraced the warmth of the empty restaurant. The steamy windows looked out on to the deserted quayside. She scanned the tick-list menu and was more than happy to order chicken souvlaki, salad, fried potatoes and a small carafe of wine. As the only customer, she welcomed the chance to make small-talk with the waitress.

Whilst she waited for her food, she took out her notebook. Sipping the cold, yellow wine she recognised the fresh citrus and herb flavours of the Vilana grapes which grew so vigorously on her land. It reminded her of a crucial decision she had yet to make. The neglected grapes were still providing a cash crop; of course, once she had thinned them out, the vines would be more productive and of better quality. There would then be more space to plant new varieties with which she hoped to develop more premium wines. But the new varieties of grape would take at least three years before they were ready for harvest. She knew her father and grandfather understood this, but she was eager to see the vineyard turn a profit so she would not be a drain on their resources.

As she ate, Chloe punched figures into the calculator on her phone, noting down her projections for various planting plans. Creating the new wines was not just about money. Since university, it had been her ambition to make wine which stood alongside those from the best producers in the world. Now she had her own vineyard, maybe she could do it here in Crete.

She thought how her father and mother had managed to craft their award-winning sparkling wine. It had taken patience, skill and no small amount of risk.

The waitress cleared away before putting some sliced apple and a karafaki of raki on the table. Chloe poured herself a glass and took a sip. It reminded her of the first time she had tasted it sitting with her father by the lake in Agios Nikolaos. When the bill arrived, Chloe couldn't believe how cheap the meal was. If she ate simply, she thought, she could survive on very little here.

Once the building work was finished she could afford to live on a modest income until the new varieties of grape were ready for harvest.

Outside, the wind blew through her and she was grateful to see a taxi at the rank to take her home. Back at the apartment, she set light to kindling and made a fire with the logs her landlady had left stacked beside the fireplace. She drew her chair close to the grate and perused the figures in her notebook. If she was frugal, maybe she could reduce the percentage of Vilana vines even more, perhaps to a third of the area, leaving her more space to grow the new varieties. It was risky. She looked at the time. It was still early evening in England. She dialled her father's number.

If Chloe could have caught glimpse of her father's face she would have seen him grinning when she told him what she was planning. It was exactly what he would have done and he gave his enthusiastic approval to her proposals.

The weekend went slowly. Chloe was impatient for the work to get started. She slept little on Sunday night and the day was just breaking as she set off up the track to the vineyard on Monday morning. She walked up to the boundary and back down to the roofless walls of the house and winery. She kept checking the time and was about to ring the contractors when she caught sight of the first of the vans driving up the mountain road.

Her impatience for the work to get started was replaced by a flurry of activity. Chloe felt pulled in two directions as each of the contractors wanted advice on her plans for the land and buildings at the same time. She assumed a calm authority, giving precise instructions to the workers doing the groundworks first. A mistake made with their machinery would prove costly. In the meantime, the builders set to work clearing the plants which had encroached on the buildings. As each hour went by, more and more of the old house revealed itself.

*

Over the following days, Chloe was careful to keep a close eye on the workers. Section by section she told them which vines to uproot and discard before weeding and rotavating the earth. They learnt to consult her if they had any doubts, and as time went on she came to trust them. Some days work came on apace, while on others progress appeared slow. Within a week though, the work clearing the land and constructing the trellises was complete. In her mind's eye Chloe could see the vineyard she longed for taking shape.

Now she could focus her attention on pruning the remaining vines, training them up the new trellises and getting ready for spring when she would plant her new crop varieties. Tending to the vineyard, during the day her mind was taken off the work on the house, but every evening the foreman would show her what had been done, and soon she was amazed to see a lorry loaded with joists, battens, rafters and tiles manoeuvring into the courtyard.

She went with Georgia to look for a truck. Her father had been happy for her to buy a new vehicle, but in the recession there were so many second-hand 4x4s available that she opted for one that was barely a year old for much less money. She was pleased to save on the capital expenditure, and being able to return the hire car improved her cash flow no end.

When the roofs were complete, Chloe could envisage how her home would look. Concrete floors were poured, windows and doors fitted before the electricians and plumbers put in the services. When the plasterers arrived to render the walls outside and in, Chloe could hardly wait until the stucco was dry so she could start decorating. She sanded the doors and windows before priming, undercoating and painting them the traditional deep blue favoured in the village.

The weeks and months flew by and in early May a lorry arrived with the stock of new vines she had ordered and she had to turn her attention back to the land. She put every plant in its allotted place and long days were spent digging and nurturing the earth, watering in and training the young vines. Chloe was relieved to get all the planting done by the middle of the month as it was getting hotter and hotter by the day, and every afternoon she fell into the habit of taking a siesta. She was proud of what she had achieved and sometimes walked to the top of the vineyard to sit on the drystone wall and look down at the neat rows of vines running down the hillside.

Now she had to concentrate on preparing for the autumn harvest. The winery must take precedence if she was to process her own crop of village wine. She sent videos of her progress to her parents and grandparents, and her father reminded her of the stainless steel vats and oak casks he had offered her. Interested to see all the developments, he suggested that he drive over in a van and deliver them himself in June. He could order the destalkers, presses and pipework from his suppliers which he would then fit for her. Chloe was not sure she believed him when he told her it would be more economical than her buying the equipment in Crete, but she kept her thoughts to herself; she would love to see him and was grateful for his offer to oversee the installation of the equipment.

She emailed him drawings of the winery, and he replied with plans of where the electric power sockets, water supplies and drainage should all be situated in readiness for the installation. The builders now turned their attention to laying the stone floor in the winery and running in the services specified by Michalis in preparation for his arrival.

It was with a mixture of pride and excitement that Chloe awaited the visit of her father. She had swept and washed the empty winery before doing her daily inspection of her vines. As she walked between the rows of trellises she kept glancing at the road winding up the mountainside. It was mid-morning when she spotted a large van beginning its climb from Elounda. She ran down the hillside to meet it, arriving in the courtyard outside the house as the vehicle pulled in. She was overjoyed to see her father was not alone. Sitting alongside him was her grandfather and another man who she recognised as Steve, the technician from their vineyard in Kent.

Chloe rushed towards them, hugging her father and grandfather in turn and shaking Steve's hand.

'What a lovely surprise. I'm so happy to see you all,' Chloe gushed, beaming.

'Well, as we were making the crossing from Brindisi it made sense to stop over with Dad, and he decided he'd join us to see how you were getting on.'

'You must be tired and starving. Shall we go and find something to eat?' Chloe asked.

'We had a sleep and something to eat on the ferry from Piraeus. Let's get unloaded first.' Chloe did not argue; she could see that her father was bursting to take a look around the buildings and the vineyard, and she was proud to show them to him. With the help of the builders they unloaded the van. The vats, casks and piping were carefully lowered to the ground and carried to the new winery ready for installation. Chloe gave them a guided tour of the house, her father and grandfather amazed at the transformation in the building. Then she took them outside into the vineyard.

She saw the smile on her grandfather's face as he looked closely at the new varieties of grapes she had so lovingly planted, the Thrapsathira, Mandilari and Kotsifali alongside the Vidiano she had rescued and further supplemented with new plants. As they strolled through the rows higher up the hillside she watched as her father and grandfather examined the clusters of young Vilana grapes which she would harvest that autumn.

'You've worked wonders here, but I knew you would,' said Michalis. Chloe felt a sense of pride at her father's approval. 'Now let's go and get some food. Then the three of us can book in to our hotel and come back and make a start installing the equipment.'

Chloe was eager to show them the new truck. Michalis and Panagiotis sat alongside her in the cab, while Steve climbed in the back. As his daughter drove around the bends on the narrow road, Michalis looked out over the olive groves and smallholdings and at the bay below stretching out to the canal and Mirabello beyond. Little had changed since the childhood he had spent there. Chloe braked hard to avoid a chicken in the road. How quickly and well his daughter had fitted in to her new life in the village, he thought, and the progress she had made with the vineyard was incredible.

He had been impressed that she had taken the decision to plant more of the new varieties for the future and was content to live on a restricted income for a few years to achieve her goal of eventually producing a range of premium wines. The businessman inside him had only one concern. Was the vineyard large enough to ever provide a really good income? He was convinced Chloe could make a living, but would his daughter be able to produce enough wine to turn it into a flourishing concern which would satisfy her ambitions as a winemaker? It was some years before they need worry about such things.

Chloe spotted a parking space on the quay and swung the truck into it as Michalis pushed his thoughts aside. He could see that his daughter was happy with her new life, and for the time being, that was all that mattered.

Later that afternoon, the three men shuffled the vats into position and lifted the crusher, press and de-stalker to the spots Chloe had marked out for them on the new stone floor. The empty barrels were then rolled into place, racked and chocked with wedges. The following day they began plumbing in the water supply and the pipes through which the juice would flow from the presses and crushers to the vats. Valves, pumps and gauges and a filtration unit were all bolted and soldered into place, and within three days the system was ready to test.

With the winery fully equipped, the business became very real for Chloe. She was delighted by the work her father, grandfather and Steve had done and excited by the prospect of using the equipment to produce her first village wine.

Less than a week after their arrival, Chloe was waving everyone goodbye. She was sad to see them go, but also fired up by the prospect of the times ahead. She could now get on with finishing the house. Whilst the builders were snagging, she went shopping in Agios Nikolaos for furniture, bedding and kitchen utensils.

In the evenings she worked on designs for the branding of the wine she would make from the autumn harvest. If all went well, the young white would be ready for market in spring the following year, in time for the reopening of local tavernas for the new tourist season. She sourced suppliers for the boxes she hoped to sell to the bars and restaurants and for the bottles she would try to sell wholesale to shops. She knew she would have to work hard to establish herself in the market, but was convinced the wine would be good and was prepared to sell it at a competitive price. She was intent on being patient and did not try to pre-promote her wine but would let its quality and taste speak for itself when she had made it. She felt encouraged by Alexander's support; her new friend had announced he would serve her wine in his taverna, so confident was he that it would be of good quality.

The day her bed was due to arrive, Chloe was buzzing. That morning she handed the keys of her apartment back to her landlady and walked up the track to the vineyard to await the delivery. With the bed in place in her newly painted bedroom, she unwrapped the sheets she had bought and made it up. She had moved into her new home. Making herself a cup of coffee she sat outside at the patio table on the terrace which looked out onto the gravelled courtyard and beyond up the mountainside.

She allowed herself a moment of satisfaction at all she had achieved. It was July, and the sun was already high in the sky. Finishing her coffee, she walked up to the first rows of immature vines. Happy to see that they had all taken, she bent down and tied a young tendril to the trellis. The fact that the infant vines had established themselves in the earth boded well for the future.

Higher up the hillside the mature plants had been thinned and were flourishing, reaching out along the stakes and wires, bunches of grapes nestling in the leaves. Chloe pulled at a yellow fruit but it took some force to separate it from the cluster. It was still small and as she put it in her mouth, she could taste the bitterness. It would be some time before the crop would be ready but, if all went well, it looked as though the harvest would be plentiful.

Reaching the wall, she looked up the mountain through the overgrown vines and weeds on Thanos' land. In the six months it had been for sale she had seen a few people who seemed to be foreigners looking around the property, but none had stayed long. For a moment she let down her defences and a thought of what might have been entered her head before she turned back down the mountainside.

Each day would follow the same pattern. She drank a coffee outside, before walking through the vineyard, inspecting the vines and pulling up any weeds she found growing between the lines of trellis. Tasting the grapes, she could tell they were getting sweeter. She could feel them growing plumper in her hand and the stems browning almost imperceptibly day by day.

By the end of August she could sense it was almost time, but she held her nerve. She could still taste more bitterness than the hint of acidity she wanted in the flesh and the seeds. Now she would wake earlier, drinking her coffee as the sun rose before testing the grapes at the dawn of the new day. She had all her equipment ready, a stack of crates and her secateurs. The harvest would be hard work on her own, but it would allow her to select the grapes as they ripened, each day picking those that were ready to be pressed. That would ensure the best quality of young wine and allow her to assess the magnitude of the task for following years as the size of the harvest grew.

One day in early September the day had come. The grapes felt plump to her touch, almost ready to burst with juice. Chloe plucked one from a bunch and put it in her mouth. She could taste the sweetness of the juice on her tongue, tempered by a hint of acidity. She walked higher up the mountainside, stopping to test her crop as she went. It was time to begin the harvest.

After picking her quota for the day, she had to carry the crates to the winery and empty them into the de-stalker and press before the must was decanted into the vats to begin fermentation. Exhausted but excited, she opened the tap on the first vat and poured a glass of the juice. Give it time, she thought, and it would provide her with the perfect young wine she was hoping for.

For two weeks she walked the rows of vines selecting bunches ripe for picking, and each day she phoned her father. He too was in the midst of the harvest and they chatted about how it was going and the quality and quantity of their respective yields. He advised her how the crushed stalks, pips and skins could be stored to put back into the earth to fertilize next year's crop, and how long the bottling and boxing process might take when the wine was ready in the spring.

By the end of the fortnight the harvest was in. The yellow-brown pomace residue had been stored in plastic containers and the grape must filled two of the stainless steel vats. Chloe was worn out, but her pleasure at completing her first harvest outweighed the aching she felt in her body. After the last grapes had been pressed, she phoned her father to let him know the job was complete.

Michalis was happy that the quantity of juice that Chloe's grapes had rendered was as good as could have been expected. She could tell he was proud of her, and sensed he was happy to have this connection with the island which was so big a part of his heritage. As she hung up the phone, she could feel the exhaustion of the last few weeks overtake her, but inside she was fighting it with the elation of her achievements. She was too exhilarated to sleep and too tired to cook herself a meal.

Since the grape harvest had begun she had not been to the village taverna and as she walked through the door, Alexander greeted her as though she had been away for years. It was late in the evening and the taverna was busy. There were no tables free but Alexander introduced her to a group of walkers who made space for her. One of them was an English artist called Amy who lived in the village. She had seen the work that had been done on the vineyard on her walks in the hills, and had even taken photographs from which she intended to do a painting.

The two women fell into conversation and Amy listened, fascinated as Chloe explained the history of the vineyard and her efforts to restore its fortunes. Amy loved the young woman's enthusiasm as she spoke of her first harvest and about the vines she had rescued and the new ones she had planted. Chloe was thrilled when her new friend offered to help design labels for the bottles of her first vintage.

As the locals began to drift away and the food orders stopped, Alexander joined them at the table. 'Now the harvest is over, we should make raki,' he said enthusiastically. 'I'm sure I can borrow a still, if not we can make one.'

As for so long the only vineyard had been Tassos', and he kept himself to himself, the village no longer had a licence to produce raki. 'We don't need to worry about that. The most important thing is to get a still,' insisted Alexander.

Chapter 15

AS THANOS ROUNDED the corner he caught sight of a fire on the hillside. He stopped. Staring into the darkness he could see it was coming from Chloe's land. He could make out the sound of a lyra drifting down the mountainside on the cool breeze and he turned up the collar on his coat. He would take the road up to the house rather than the track so he could go unnoticed. The last thing he wanted was to see Chloe, frightened it would ignite the feelings he had for her. Though it had been almost a year since he'd seen her, forgetting the girl who had saved his life had proved almost as impossible as any relationship between them might be.

His dream of setting up his own taverna in Loutro, or anywhere else, was no closer to being a reality as he could not sell the property. The recession had bitten hard and, in all the months it had been on the market, no offers had been made. The cost of restoring the house, digging up the vineyard and turning it over to an olive grove or even a smallholding was proving prohibitive to prospective buyers when money was in such short supply.

He was long since back on his feet and since the spring had been working again in his aunt's taverna but still felt he was a drain on his parents' tiny pension. More than that, though, he was longing to fulfil his creative ambitions, to make a name for himself. He had to find a way forward. Maybe he needed to do some sprucing up of the house to make it appeal more to a foreign buyer as a holiday home. He could at least paint it outside and in and get it in a presentable state. He had nothing to lose. One thing was for sure, it would not get done whilst he remained in Loutro.

It had been a long day. He had taken the first ferry to Chora Sfakion and caught the connecting bus to Chania on the north coast. From there he had taken the long bus ride to Heraklion then on to Agios Nikolaos and changed again for the local service to Elounda. All he wanted was to get to the house and fall asleep and begin work in the morning, completing it quickly, to make a sale at the best price he could achieve. As he crept along the wall near the buildings at the bottom of Chloe's land he could make out the fire and hear music and laughter, and see the shadows of people dancing. He hastened his step uphill to his grandfather's house, turned the key in the door and fumbled for the light switch.

*

Alexander had been as good as his word. It had been no problem to borrow a still from his uncle, and a date had been set for the *rakokazano*, when they would get together to make the raki. It was November by the time the pomace had fermented enough, the *moesta* ready to be distilled. Alexander took charge of both the makeshift still and the grill which he had brought from his taverna. Friends and other villagers invited by Alexander had all contributed to the feast, bringing salads, tzatziki, bread, cheese and hummus to accompany the pork and chicken souvlaki sizzling over the coals. Large plastic containers of wine were passed around until the first drops of raki began to drip from the still.

One of the locals had a bouzouki and Alexander had brought his lyra. As the wine flowed the music rippled across the mountainside. It took little encouragement for the guests to dance and Chloe was dragged into the line which wound its way around the courtyard and in between the rows of vines stretching up the hillside. Taking a break to catch her breath, she sat down and watched her new friends eating, drinking and dancing.

She looked up: the sky was black, twinkling with thousands of stars. She felt so small and somehow the thought comforted her. A lone goat bell tinkled somewhere high above and she scanned the impenetrable darkness of the looming hills. Below she could make out the lights of the causeway as though floating across the inky waters of the bay, crossing to the isle of Kalydon. She could see no lights from fishing boats, but the harbour of Elounda glowed warm in the chill night air.

She watched as Alexander filled a container with the first of the clear liquid from the still. 'This is too strong to drink. It is almost pure alcohol.' When he was satisfied it had reached the right strength, he handed her a glass. 'The first of the drinkable raki for you to taste. *Yammas*!'

Chloe sipped, and the comforting hot trickle ran down her throat and deep inside her. All around, the guests were clapping as Alexander poured drinks for them in turn. Chloe closed her eyes and thought she couldn't be any happier. Re-opening them, she caught a glimpse of a light turn on up the mountainside. It was dim and in no time was extinguished. Sure she had not imagined it, she waited until people had dispersed to start dancing again, then unnoticed she disappeared into the shadows of the vineyard. Slowly she began to climb through the trellised rows uphill. Reaching the wall, she climbed over and pushed her way through the tangle of plants towards Thanos' house.

That night when he opened the door of his grandfather's house, Thanos could not have felt more self-conscious. In front of him stood the beautiful young woman he had so hoped to avoid. He knew he had been ungracious not contacting her since he had left hospital, but a combination of guilt about their families' shared legacy and his misgivings about entering into a long-distance relationship had held him back. He didn't even know if she liked him or had just cared for him out of kindness or duty.

'Aren't you going to invite me in?'

Politeness allowed him no alternative, and seeing Chloe now rekindled the feelings he had been so wary of.

As she entered, he was tongue-tied. He knew that he had behaved badly towards her but was struggling to find a way to make amends.

Chloe had not had time to unravel her feelings. When she saw the light in the house, something had drawn her towards it. She should have been angry with Thanos for his ingratitude.

Thanos broke the awkward silence. 'I would offer you a drink. But I've only just arrived and have nothing in the house.'

'We've got plenty at my place. We're having a *rakokazano*. The first batch has just started to flow from the still. You're welcome to join us.' Chloe could see the disquiet written on his face. 'We've got wine if you'd prefer it?' she said, trying to make him feel at ease.

For a moment a smile flashed across his handsome features and his eyes met hers. At once he turned away and his face returned to his impassive look. 'Thank you, but no. I don't think your friends would want to see me.'

'You are not your grandfather. You are not a fascist sympathiser. You did not start the fire or steal the land from my family!' Chloe stunned herself with the vehemence of her response. She could see the shock on Thanos' face and softened. 'Trust me, they will welcome you. Come with me, we've got food too.'

Thanos let himself be led from the house towards the glow of the fire and the sound of music and laughter. Although the night air was cold he found himself sweating. As they walked into the courtyard, in the flickering light of the fire Chloe could see Thanos wrestling with his emotions.

'This is my friend Thanos,' Chloe announced, stepping out of the shadows.

She had been right, her friends and the villagers made Thanos welcome. At first he was wary, but Chloe stayed at his side, introducing him to her guests one by one, and after some raki and wine he began to relax.

'I'll get you something to eat.' Chloe led him to the barbecue, taking a souvlaki off the grill before adding salad to the plate. 'Here, let's grab a seat indoors.'

Passing through the front door, Thanos could not believe how beautiful the house was. Last time he had seen the building it had been a wreck, destroyed by the fire his grandfather had started.

'Let's sit here.' Chloe put the plate down on the table and went to the fridge to get some wine to top up their glasses.

'Is this your wine?' Thanos asked.

'No,' Chloe laughed, 'it won't be ready until the spring.'

'As you can probably tell, I'm no expert.'

'But you're a chef,' Chloe jokingly chided him, noticing his dark eyes light up as he relaxed into her company.

'I would be if I had a restaurant. I work a bit in my aunt and uncle's taverna, but it's not the same. That's why I need to sell the house and the vineyard. But no-one's interested in buying. I've come back to try and put the house into better shape so perhaps a foreign buyer might be interested. In this recession, nobody wants land. At least not as it is at the moment.' Chloe saw Thanos' face fall.

'I could help you perhaps clear the land a bit too.' The words came out before Chloe realised what she was saying. 'Now the harvest is in and with the new vines in the earth I'll have some spare time.'

As soon as Chloe had made the offer, she could see Thanos withdraw into himself. 'I'm tired. I'd better get back to the house. Thank you for this evening.' He stood.

'You haven't answered me. Would you like me to help you?'

'Sleep on it. You may feel different in the morning. *Kalinichta.*' Thanos turned and slipped through the door.

It was the early hours before Chloe climbed into her bed. But although tired, she couldn't sleep. She tossed and turned, telling herself that a relationship with Thanos would be doomed to failure. He was too distant and hung up on the past, and anyway he would be moving away as soon as he could get rid of the property. But something would not allow her let go of her impetuous offer to help him.

The following morning she was up early, busy tidying away the remains of the party from the night before and wasting the hours and minutes until she felt it a reasonable time to head up the hillside. She loaded tools into the new truck and took the short drive up the mountain road to Thanos' house.

As she approached the front door, Thanos opened it. 'I got us some breakfast. I couldn't sleep so I went down to Elounda to get some supplies. Come in.' Standing aside, he held the door as Chloe went inside. The house was a mess, but in the middle of the room a table had been spread with a cloth and laid with a selection of fruit, a jar of honey, a bowl of nuts and a tub of yoghurt.

'I hope this is OK?' The corners of Thanos' mouth turned upwards and Chloe caught his eye. This time he held her gaze.

'It looks lovely. You should smile more often. It suits you.' Chloe's sparkling eyes put him at ease.

'I'm sorry, I've been behaving like an idiot, haven't I?' He didn't give Chloe time to answer, afraid of what she might say. 'Can we start again? If you can forgive me for being so ungrateful, especially after all you've done for me?'

Chloe smiled and took her seat at the table.

*

The air was cold and digging the ground was hard work. Chloe naturally gravitated to working on the land, while Thanos worked on improving the house.

By the end of the first week the winter sun held more warmth and Chloe began to make more progress clearing the old vines and turning over the soil. She looked forward to lunchtimes and the delicious food Thanos would prepare for her: roast pork, the meat melting off the bone, served with herby potatoes drizzled in olive oil and lemon juice; or spicy soutzoukakia in tomato sauce on a bed of creamy mashed potato. It warmed her to think that maybe he was trying to impress her a little. If it was dry they would eat outside the old house, or if raining, inside by the fire Thanos lit in the grate. At first lunchtimes were short, each of them keen to get back to working on their respective tasks, but as time went by their daily chats grew longer.

Over the days and weeks, Thanos opened up about his guilt over his grandfather's seizure of Chloe's family land, as well as how protective he was of his mother after all she had been through as a child and then his parents losing everything in the ongoing recession. Strangely, the more he unburdened himself of his worries, the more his confidence returned.

In the evening, Chloe would go back to the comfort of her new home. After she had showered she would go to the winery to check on the progress of her young wine. Twice a week she phoned her mother and father. Chloe had told them she was helping her neighbour prepare his land and the house for sale.

Charlotte noticed how day by day her daughter had grown happier and with her friendship with Thanos and other people in the village, she was less concerned about her daughter being lonely.

Michalis was proud of his daughter and what she had achieved. When he heard that the land on the next door property was still up for sale, increasingly it occurred to him the perfect solution to any doubts he had about the future of the business was staring him in the face. 'I was having the very same thoughts,' said his father when Michalis phoned him with his idea.

The evening Michalis called his daughter to explain their proposal to put in a further investment to buy the neighbouring land, her reaction was not as enthusiastic as he expected. But she thanked him and said she would think about it.

Of course her father was right, it made perfect sense. So why did she feel so reluctant to put forward the offer to Thanos? She thought long and hard, and realised that her reticence was because she did not want Thanos to leave. Her feelings for him had grown so strong. But the thought that she might withhold an offer which would secure both of their futures brought Chloe to her senses. All Thanos wanted was to get the money to start his taverna near where his mother and father lived in the west. If she bought the land, it would make his house easier to sell to a foreigner, and the extra hectares of vines she could grow would make her long-term business secure.

That night she churned over thoughts of how the new business model would work and how she could use the extra land to maximize the quality of the Vilana grapes, allowing her to plant more of the new varieties that spring in the ground she had already cultivated. In her dreams she imagined tours around the vineyard and winery, wine tastings and even a restaurant which would make the vineyard a destination. She imagined her new wines finding a market all over Greece and beyond; the business she had begun to build would thrive and become recognised for its fine wines.

The following morning as she drank her coffee in the courtyard, she wrote down her projections and what she thought would be a fair offer to make Thanos. Somehow, in the cold light of the new dawn, her dreams of the night before did not fill her with such optimism and her figures fluctuated between an over-generous offer which would more than fulfil Thanos' dream or one it would be impossible for him to accept so he would remain. Pulling herself together, she determined to be professional. Although she could now consider herself to be friends with Thanos, she had no reason to believe that there was anything more to their relationship than that. She pored over the figures in her notebook and came up with a sum she considered reasonable, then rounded it up to ensure it was more than fair.

As Chloe worked on the mountainside that morning, she found it difficult to concentrate. She had decided to broach the subject over lunch. Part of her wanted to get the conversation over and done with but another side of her wanted to delay it as long as possible. As they sat down to eat lunch, she took a deep breath and launched her proposal to buy the land. Thanos looked shocked.

It was everything he wanted, he thought. So why did he not feel happy? He had thought when Chloe had volunteered to help him that it was a gesture of friendship. He was confused by his feelings.

'Thank you.' At first that was all he could think of to say. 'I had not yet worked out the price for the land without the house, but your offer seems generous. Give me some time to think it over.' Thanos felt the distance between them open up as they sat eating in silence, Chloe uncomfortable at his reaction. Through the afternoon they both applied themselves to their tasks, both discomfited by their feelings and unsure why.

Sofia could sense the sadness in her son's voice when he phoned that evening to tell her the news about the offer. Her intuition told her that her son had been wrestling with his emotions about Chloe. 'Why don't you tell her how you feel?'

Thanos went silent. Were the feelings he had for Chloe so obvious to his mother? He had been set on opening a taverna close to his parents so maybe he could supplement their depleted savings and look after them as they got older. When he admitted this to his mother, and his chagrin at how his grandfather had treated Chloe's family, he could tell she was upset.

'I'm truly sorry if my guilt has rubbed off on you,' Sofia told her son. 'I have tried, believe me, to wipe the memory of my father from my mind. It is hard for me to forget, but you must not let the past ruin your life.'

She laughed off any suggestion that she and Milos needed his support. 'When you have your own taverna we will hardly see you anyway, and with one less mouth to feed we will get by just fine. Elounda is on the same island,' she told him. 'Don't rush into any decisions, but if you think you love her, don't let her go.'

Afraid he would lose his nerve, Thanos put on his coat and stepped out into the darkness, making his way through the vineyard to the boundary wall. The stones were cold to the touch as he climbed over and walked between the neatly pruned rows of vines towards Chloe's house. As he got closer he slowed his pace, before speeding up again, realising if he hesitated he might lose his resolve. Seeing the house was in darkness, he thought of turning back but took a deep breath and knocked. It seemed an eternity before a light went on and Chloe opened the door, her slim body and beautiful face framed in the warm glow from inside.

'I'm sorry,' was all he could think of to say, looking to the floor.

Chloe stepped forward, took his head in her hands and kissed him. 'You'd better come in.'

Epilogue

2024

MICHALIS STEPPED OUT of the warmth of the house. The wind bit through his coat and the rain stung his face. He wrapped a protective arm around his wife as she got into the back seat of the taxi beside Chloe and Thanos, then settled himself in the front. As the car pulled away, the driver wiped condensation from the windscreen.

'Filthy day,' remarked Michalis. 'Are you three alright in the back?'

Thanos leant forward and tried to peer out the windscreen into the sodden murk of the winter evening. All he could see were the occasional headlights of cars coming the other way on the narrow country roads. He felt Chloe reach for his hand and settled back into the seat. Why was he so nervous? It was his first time away from Greece, but he had enjoyed the journey to Kent and had been made to feel welcome by Chloe's parents who he knew well from their regular visits to Epano Elounda.

'Don't worry, the kids will be fine,' reassured Chloe. 'They're fast asleep, and even if they do wake up they love Steve and Evie. They'll be no problem.'

'I know, love.' Thanos kissed her on the cheek. Even in the darkness he could sense her beauty. She was wearing her long blond hair up and he could make out the pendant earring as she turned her neck towards him, moving closer and squeezing his hand. He felt the golden bracelet, the pearl grapes grazing his wrist. Why was he so on edge? It was not he who was up for the award.

It had been something of a shock when Chloe received the letter. Just four years into the production of her premium blended white, it had been shortlisted for a prize for Best New Wine to be presented at a prestigious award ceremony at a London hotel. Michalis and Charlotte had also been nominated for their English sparkling. Thanos was so proud of Chloe, and desperate for her to win. Her parents were old hands at this and their wine was already a multi-award-winning product. Chloe had said she didn't care if she won or not. But Thanos knew that success would mean more to her than she let on. It would validate her determination and hard work, and repay her parents' and grandparents' faith in her.

The country lanes gave way to busier roads and then a motorway before joining a stream of traffic heading towards the centre of the city. Even when Thanos had lived in Athens he could not remember having seen so many people, coats wrapped around them against the cold, sheltering under umbrellas as they hastened their way towards shops and underground stations. Outside the brightly lit entrance to a towering hotel, a liveried man opened the doors of the taxi. Another man in uniform ushered them into the comfort of the plush foyer where they took off their coats and queued for the cloakroom.

After a drinks reception they were seated with another group at a table in the banqueting suite where they were served a three-course meal of duck terrine, chicken ballotine and chocolate torte before the awards ceremony began.

When it came to the Best New Wine category and the results were announced, Chloe could see the disappointment on

Thanos' face when her wine received a Silver. She, however, was beaming, and her parents were jubilant at her success. Thanos did not know how to respond so he just kissed her.

The taxi picked them up at midnight and it was more than an hour later by the time they arrived home. Steve and Evie assured them the children had not stirred and after congratulating Chloe on her success, they took their leave.

'I'm ready for bed too,' said Michalis, yawning.

'We'll see you in the morning.' Charlotte followed her husband towards the door. 'Well done, Chloe. We're so proud of you. Goodnight darling, goodnight Thano.'

In the sitting room, Chloe was still animated by her success.

'Shall we have a nightcap before we go up?' Thanos suggested.

'Why not. It's not every day you get recognised as a prize-winning winemaker. I'll get us a bottle of the wine in question from the fridge.' Chloe laughed heading for the kitchen.

Alone, Thanos nervously checked the pocket of his waistcoat. Chloe returned, handing him a chilled bottle and a corkscrew. She put two glasses on the coffee table as Thanos pulled the cork and poured.

'*Yammas*, to a wonderful winemaker. And to a wonderful wine from Crete.' He raised his glass and clinked it on Chloe's.

At that moment, Chloe thought she could not be happier; then she saw Thanos drop on one knee and pull a small box from his pocket.

'Will you marry me?'

Chloe had never been so certain of anything in her life. She nodded several times before she could get the words out. 'Yes, yes I will.'

Relieved, Thanos got to his feet and Choe kissed him.

'Get another two glasses,' she said leaving the room and running upstairs to tell her parents the news.

*

Thanos loosened his tie as he stood beside the wall at the edge of the large terrace which surrounded the taverna. He looked and saw Chloe in her white wedding dress, laughing as she chatted with their friends. Turning round, he could see their two young children playing beneath the long table where the wedding guests were seated. He stopped himself from crossing the terrace to the outdoor kitchen to help serve the food which he had insisted on preparing for the occasion. He was under strict instructions from Chloe not to work during the reception and leave it to the staff from the taverna. Chloe caught sight of him watching her and waved, beaming as he waved back.

Chloe never did buy the vineyard. From that first kiss it had seemed natural that their fortunes would be conjoined. When Thanos had moved into the house down the hill, the couple worked tirelessly to turn his house into a taverna. They built an outside kitchen with wood-fired brick ovens and charcoal grills and the large terrace which surrounded the building where the wedding guests now sat eating and drinking. At the top table Thanos could see his mother laughing as she chatted with Charlotte, and his father deep in conversation with Michalis. He smiled at the irony of how Sofia and Michalis' fateful relationship all that time ago had brought them here.

Approaching their nineties, Panagiotis and Calliope had insisted that they come, and sat together in companionable silence, their faces radiating happiness as they shared in the joy of their granddaughter's wedding. Panagiotis had long retired and the business in Puglia had been merged with the vineyards in Kent and Epano Elounda, with his manager now looking after affairs in Italy.

When her grandchildren had been born, Sofia had overcome her reluctance to return to the land where she had lived as a child. Now, during harvest time, she and Milos would come and help look after their grandkids while Chloe was busy managing the pickers.

Since the fine wines had been developed, Chloe had established tours of the vineyard and winery, ending with tastings and a meal in the taverna which was Thanos' domain. It too had been a huge success, having a reputation for only serving organic produce which came from the land or sea within a few kilometres of the restaurant.

Alexander had brought his lyra and took to the stage alongside Phoebe and Alice, two musicians who Chloe had met who lived in the village. As dusk began to settle over the mountainside the music struck up. The children came out from under the tables, dragging their parents onto the space that had been cleared on the terrace to dance. The sound of the lyra wove its way through the vineyard, winding round the trellises like the tendrils of the vines and down past the house and winery, through the olive trees to the waters of the bay.

Chloe reached for Thanos' hand. From the top table she picked up a bottle of her wine and two glasses and they slipped away into the shadows and downhill to where the wall had once stood, all signs of it long gone beneath the tilled earth and the rows of vines, the stones used to make the foundations of the terrace where the wedding guests were now celebrating. Up the hill they could hear the music and laughter coming from the brightly lit taverna and below them they could make out the white walls of the house which was the family home.

Chloe gave a glass to her husband and poured them both a drink. She looked deep into Thanos' eyes and held up her glass. 'To us, and our Cretan vineyard.

Did You Enjoy This Book?

If you liked reading this book and have time, any review on www.amazon.co.uk or www.amazon.com would be appreciated and it would be good to meet up with any readers on my facebook page at www.facebook.com/richardclarkbooks.